Harvey Unna &
Stephen Durbridge Ltd

14 Beaumont Mews
Marylebone High Street
London W1N 4HE

Telephone 01-935 8589

Gentle Folk

By the same author

From The City, From The Plough
There's No Home
Rosie Hogarth
With Hope, Farewell
The Human Kind
The Golden Princess
Queen of The East
Seeing Life
The Lowlife
Strip Jack Naked
King Dido
The In-Between Time

Gentle Folk

a novel by

Alexander Baron

FOR NICHOLAS

SBN 333 18649 4

First published 1976 by
MACMILLAN LONDON LIMITED
*4 Little Essex Street London WC2R 3LF
and Basingstoke
Associated companies in New York, Dublin
Melbourne, Johannesburg and Delhi*

Printed in Great Britain by
THE GARDEN CITY PRESS LIMITED
Letchworth, Hertfordshire SG6 1JS

One

Richard Latt stepped down from the train and looked
up and down the platform. He was in the shade of the
canopy but beyond and above was an ocean of pure
pale blue sky from which heat poured down. The wind-
less air was hot and heavy against him. He fanned
himself with the straw hat he carried in his right hand.

"Porter, sir?"

He gave the man his big gladstone bag. Only three
other people had got down from the train and they
were all passing the ticket barrier by now. No-one else
was in sight but the guard and the driver leaning out
of the locomotive cab. "I was to be met here. I'm going
to a Mr Menant. Do you know—?"

"Mr Menant's motor-car—" The porter's r's were
rural. "Yes, sir."

The porter walked up the ramp to the exit. By the
time Richard had given up his ticket and caught up with
him, the porter had handed the gladstone bag to the
driver of a Daimler motor-car, an upright, gleaming
affair of maroon and brass. Richard said, "Thank
you," to the porter and dismissed him with a sixpenny
piece. To the driver, "Good morning."

"Morning, sir." The driver was in his thirties, a com-
pact, alert man. His glove-fitting dark grey uniform was
plain except for sprigs of braid round the halfpenny-
sized leather buttons each quartered like a hot-cross bun.

5

A similar button was sewed like a soldier's badge in the front centre of his grey peaked cap. He opened the rear door. "Mr Richard Latt, will it be, sir?"

"Yes."

Richard climbed into the car. As he settled into the comfortable back seat—

"I should have recognised you, sir. Miss Portia told me."

"Ah." Richard had come out of the station with a skip of hope-then-disappointment in his breast.

The driver slammed Richard's door and got into his own seat. He put his hands on various controls. "Fair hair, rather red face, she said, and a young man, her age."

To this Richard could only say, "Ah."

He had advanced views. After all, it was 1911 and, if one was young, one was advanced; at least in the circle to which Portia had introduced Richard. He did not, however, know how to talk to members of what he was careful not to call the lower classes when they addressed him in this brisk, man-to-man way, underlining the unflattering hint in Portia's description. Richard had chosen to live and work among the poor. A few of them professed the same advanced views as his, but all were doggedly respectful.

"Another scorcher, sir."

"Yes."

"Seems no end to it."

"No." The great drought was in its second month.

"Farmers are going mad. Still, promises well for the cricket."

"Cricket?"

"Bank Holiday Monday, sir. We have it every August.

6

We get up a team at the house to play the village. Of course we've got the estate chaps for our team as well. Plenty of muscle there. Not much brain, though. I'm a Londoner myself."

"Oh, yes?"

"Do you play, sir?"

Richard simulated a laugh. "When I have to."

They crossed a bridge over the River Ouse and turned right out of Lewes. The road ran by the side of the river. The car gathered speed. The driver relaxed into his seat as if he were part of it. His smooth shaven face looked cool as marble. His gaze ahead was serene. Richard felt the sweat cooling on his own cheeks and wondered if his face was as flamboyantly red as it had been when he came out of the station. The driver renewed his cheerful assault. "First time you've been to the house, sir?"

"House?" Richard uttered this stupid echo as a reflex. For all his beliefs in the rights of men, and, of course, women, it was hard to overcome the inbred feeling that a person employed by one's own sort for weekly wages should recognise certain proper limits to conversation. The man embarrassed him.

"Ashtons, sir."

"Yes. Indeed. It's my first visit."

"Fine old house, sir."

"So I hear."

"Very enjoyable, I find it." The man spoke as heartily as a guest. "Been there a year last Christmas. I was with Daimler's before then, qualified mechanic, factory-trained."

"Really?"

"Give me the tools and I could build a car like this for you."

"Really?" Richard had to admit to himself that the tide rising in his veins was one of resentment at encroachment into the privacies of his class. He leaned forward (he hoped, unobserved; but was the hope hypocritical?) to peer over the driver's shoulder.

"Only thirty miles an hour, sir. Don't worry."

"I'm not." Richard heard himself speaking curtly.

The road was narrow, running in a series of shallow, sinuous bends. On both sides were high, untidy hedges. They passed the gates of prosperous farms. Richard could see nothing on his left but the hedges, but on his right were the South Downs, the chain of long hills lying like sleeping beasts with green flanks through which the grey of chalk could be seen. The fields that stretched to the foot of the Downs bore witness to the drought; a phenomenal two months with no rain except the occasional unrelieving shower. Early-harvested, they were expanses of stubble, bleached as if the sunshine that poured unremittingly, making a dazzle of the daylight, had burned all the colour out of them. Richard was grateful for the breeze that the lowered windows admitted to stream upon his hot cheeks.

He was grateful, too, for the silence that the chauffeur kept as the wheels of the car swallowed mile after mile of road, crossroads after crossroads.

He was always grateful for silence. He had lived much of his life alone; and lately he had suffered experiences which in every lull between new happenings invaded his mind, as now. It was not only his unfortunate embarrassment with workmen but his need to deal with the tumult in his mind that made him grateful for every

8

silence. Lately, his great wish had been to be left alone. But the driver knocked down the wall of peace. "Job in a million, sir, that's what I've got." And to Richard's startled silence he replied, "Working for Mr Menant."

Richard managed to say, "Is it?"

"Yes, sir. Very generous gentleman. Known for it."

"Is he?"

"Oh, yes. And all these well-known people coming down to stay. I like that."

"Do you?"

"My word, yes. Being as near to them as I am to you? Talking? Why, sir, I've talked with Mr Asquith."

"Have you indeed?"

"Yes, sir. Mind you, he only came for lunch. Still, I mean! The Prime Minister!"

"Yes."

"And others, sir. Educational. I go in for education."

"Do you?"

"Oh, yes, sir. Books of a night. I expect you know who's coming down this weekend?"

"Yes." Mrs Menant had informed him in her letter of invitation.

"Mr F. J. Dobbs, sir. I've always wanted to meet him. F. J. Dobbs, sir. The novelist."

"Yes," a little testily. "I know about F. J. Dobbs."

"I've read many of his books, sir."

"I should think everybody has."

"Oh, yes, sir, to be sure."

They drove on. "I've read all his scientific tales, sir. Of course, he writes deeper stuff now."

"Yes. Yes."

They slowed. Ahead on their right was a lane entrance. The lane fell away sharply between immense

9

hedges as if into a mysterious pit of unknown depth. All beyond appeared to be dense treetops. The driver eased the car into the lane.

It was a strange, steep descent after that. The car would swoop down fast, even accelerating, for perhaps twenty yards then slow suddenly at a sharp bend; then another swoop down and another bend. The lane went down and down, bend after bend like an ill-drawn spiral. Richard could see nothing for the immense wild hedges and the close tree-trunks overgrown with creeper, except for an occasional cottage glimpsed through the greenery.

"House at the valley bottom, sir. Beneath the Downs." The driver couldn't help, it seemed, raising his voice somewhat, as if exulting in the swooping descent; like the Cockneys Richard had seen riding switchback railways in their holiday fairgrounds. "Nice few hundred acres there, sir. All on the flat, with the river running through it. Lovely piece of country—"

But his last words were overlaid by Richard's anguished cry as they swooped down towards a steep left-angled bend, "Look out, the child, the child!"

Richard glimpsed in profile the mystification that his cry struck into the driver's face; but the man (though he saw no child, for there was only the sharp bend of empty road in front of them, beneath an overhanging elm with a big red PRIVATE board nailed to its trunk) responded and brakes squealed; and, as the driver, worked the car round the bend, there was the boy slithering down the bank out of the hedge unable to stop, and they felt the slight dreadful bump passing through the motor-car and heard the small yelp. They had stopped.

The driver was stooping in the lane as if he had materialised out of the car. A voice – whose? – authoritative as an officer's rapped "Come on!" to Richard who for three endless seconds had sat dazed and far beyond reality in his rear seat.

"Sir!" The driver did not look round or shout but his peremptory voice carried to wherever Richard was. Richard, not yet returned to the tangible world, was aware of himself getting out of the car and going to look over the driver's shoulder.

The boy, perhaps seven years old, lay with his eyes open. There was a lot of blood to one side of him.

"Tool box," the driver said. "First-aid kit. Quick about it, sir."

Richard's body and limbs went and returned with the first-aid kit. The driver opened it and worked deftly. "All right, Charlie," he said to the boy, "you're all right. You had a close one that time. You want to look before you slide out of a hedge." He was bandaging the boy's head. "Not as bad as it looks," he said to Richard. "I was almost at a stop. Thanks to you, sir. Will you break open that packet of two-inch bandage?"

Richard's hands obeyed. The driver said, "He's Grayle the keeper's boy. Got a tough nut, haven't you, Charlie? Mudguard knocked him clear. He's got a long gash, right into his cheek. More blood than damage, though, eh, Charlie?"

The boy said weakly, "Yes, Mr Borrett."

"How would you like a drive up to the big house in my motor?" Borrett lifted the boy in his arms. Richard stood, not watching but looking far beyond, as if encased beyond the power to move in his narrow stiff collar, light grey suit and small brown shoes.

The driver made the boy comfortable in the car. He found a coat and in spite of the heat put it round the boy, with a cushion for headrest. Then he turned away from the car and said, "Sir? How did you know?"

Richard seemed not to hear. He looked down at the bright bloodstain turning brown in the white dust of the lane. He looked around him. Then he walked away from Borrett, up round the bend in the lane. He was back now where he had cried out, with the sharp jut of fifteen-foot-high hedge, the high promontory of undergrowth, between him and the scene of the accident, which was invisible once more. He stared up at the red board nailed to the tree. Then he walked back to the car.

Borrett watched him approach. "Sir," he said, "you couldn't have seen the lad."

Richard looked vaguely at him, unable to focus.

"You couldn't have heard him either. He was in the bushes," Borrett said, "not with the noise of the motor and everything. How did you know to shout?"

Richard stood as if trying to find an answer. He looked distressed. His face was a scarlet blush to the roots of his smoothed corn-blond hair. He shook his head slightly, but as if dismissing some speculation of his own. His eyes might have been scared, or wondering, or appealing. At last, without answering, he stepped back into the car. Borrett watched him for a second, then closed the rear door, climbed into his own seat and drove on.

Two

The Jacobean chimneys of Ashtons came into sight over the tops of a plantation of small trees; then the woods flitted away past the windows of the motor-car and Richard looked out across a spread of open country to the grey, handsome house with the Downs behind it.

A high estate wall now fronted the lane; not a long one, for Ashtons was a house of modest size. There was no carriage drive from the central gate to the house; only a flagstoned path between lawns. At the end of the front wall were double gates which admitted them into a drive. When they drew near to the house Borrett ignored the branch which led to the front door and continued along the side of the building. He had no intention of spoiling the guest's arrival by delivering him in company with a damaged brat.

They came to the rear of the house and stopped in a large flagstoned yard surrounded by outbuildings. Borrett squeezed three peremptory honks out of the rubber bulb of the horn. The noise scattered birds and as promptly brought two maids scampering from a door at the rear of the house. Big-eyed they gazed at Charlie Grayle and twittered exclamations.

"Come on, girls, give us a hand." Borrett was out of the car and in command as if it were habitual. "Get him into the kitchen. That's right, my loves. You, lad—" This was to a garden boy who had appeared. "Cut down on the bike and tell Doctor Ormerod to come along."

The kitchen doorway now framed a middle-aged woman servant in black. She said, "Hadn't you better ask the mistress?"

"My authority," Borrett said. "Off you go, sonny. Got any of that nice jam tart left, Mrs May? Give Charlie a slice. It's scrumptious, lad. You'll be glad I knocked you down."

Richard had stepped out of the car with a vague intention to help but he was disregarded. He noticed vaguely among the outbuildings that made three sides of the rectangle around him stables, with horses looking out over their half-doors; a garage in which stood a second car, a Delage tourer; a gate to the gardens behind the house; and what appeared from their neatly-curtained windows to be servants' quarters which were joined to the house by a newly-built covered way.

"If you please, sir—" Borrett was at Richard's elbow again. He opened the rear door of the motor-car and Richard, still a little somnambulistic, got in obediently. Borrett got into the driver's seat, started the engine, reversed the car and swung forward to drive solemnly round to the front of the building. Here he stopped, got out of the motor-car, tugged at a long, wrought-iron bell-pull on the porch which at once produced a clangour within, returned to open Richard's door and, as Richard stepped down, said, "Sorry for the delay, sir."

The door in the porch was of black wood with massive wrought-iron furniture. It fitted into a pointed arch. It was opened by a manservant who wished Richard a good morning, trusted his journey had been agreeable, gave the driver a "Good morning, Mr Borrett," and took Richard's bag.

Borrett said, "Good morning, Mr Hawker," and drove away.

Richard waited in the deep porch. The manservant was small and dapper, well on in middle age, with a sprinkle of grey in black hair. He looked like a confidential clerk. He said, "If you will kindly follow me, sir—"

Richard followed him into the hall. It was smaller than he had expected, with plain Jacobean panelling, a wide but simply-carved chimney-piece and arched doorways leading off to glimpsed rooms and corridors. There were brasses and old chests, lesser oddments, and a painting over the fire of pre-Raphaelite appearance : a phthisic maiden with long red hair gazing out of a confusion of flowers too brightly rendered. Hawker paused here to say, "Mrs Menant wished me to tell you, sir, that she is at present engaged in her work—" He added, as if he had been enjoined to do so, "—her creative work. She may not be disturbed, but looks forward to seeing you." He led on.

Mrs Menant was a lady writer. She was an old friend of Aunt Marian. Richard had met her often in town. From Aunt Marian he had learned a good deal about the house, Ashtons, and about the Menants. And of course he knew Portia.

Mr Menant did something or other in the City and he did rather well out of it. He was no magnate. His weekends – or rather, as Richard knew, his wife's weekends – were not grand affairs. A few couples were enough to fill the house. But Mrs Menant worked hard at her weekends, not without success.

He followed the manservant up a broad, shallow staircase in two flights to the first floor. There was tapestry, panelling, some fine wood carving, pictures, a vase of some Eastern sort on a corner table. The main bedrooms were here, obviously, and the master's study. His guide preceded him through an arched doorway beyond which he might have been in a different house. No more panelling or antiques; the massive, unevenly-squared main timbers of the house stood out of white-washed walls. There was a small landing and a narrow staircase, with linoleum and thin carpet under-foot. Hawker led the way along a narrow corridor past three rooms to Richard's.

It was a pleasant little room inside the steep roof. This whole row of guest rooms (as Richard assumed them to be) must once have been servants' quarters before the outbuildings had been turned to that purpose. Hawker set down the big gladstone bag and explained where the offices were. Richard knew him to mean the bathroom and w.c. Richard declined his offer to send a maid with hot water and insisted that he could unpack his own bag. He did this as soon as Hawker had gone, washed in cold water from the jug on the washstand, lay down on the bed and closed his eyes. He had much to think about.

He felt steady again after a little while, back in the material world. The bed had plain but daintily-made brass ends, a deep mattress and soft, light blankets. The floorboards were polished, with rugs, the towels soft. The wallpaper and curtains were of William Morris design, pale blue predominant. There was a dormer window in a deep recess.

Through it, to his left, he could see the front approach to the house and the wooded slope down which he had come from the Lewes road; to his right was the steep flank of a down – Long Down, of which Portia had told him; in front of him was a large rectangular garden, with yew hedges, close-mown lawns, three rows of lime trees and a lake with water lilies on its surface. Near to the lake's edge were a garden table and chairs, of lacy white-painted iron. Alone on one of the chairs, reading, was Portia.

He sluiced his face again, enjoying the cold water, combed his hair smooth, dusted his own shoes, made sure at a wall mirror that his clothes were tidy, and went downstairs.

Mrs Menant was in the hall, arranging flowers in a bowl. "Mr Latt, how nice of you to come."

They shook hands.

"How nice of you to have me."

She was one of those small thin women who seem all bone and determination. She wore a businesslike jacket and skirt of dark grey. There was no repose in her face, framed by iron-grey hair in close curls. She spoke, as always, energetically. She was not in the least like Portia.

"And how is your aunt?"

"She is well, thank you. She sends you her love."

"Dear Marian. I wish she could have come."

"She's going to Switzerland."

"I know. To walk. We used to walk in the Alps together. My goodness, the miles we walked. And how are you? I am going to call you Richard, since you are in my care. Marian has been worried about you."

"I've been much better, Mrs Menant. I – er, I say, Mrs Menant, I don't know if your chauffeur has told you—"

"My dear boy, don't worry about that. It's all seen to,

and young Charlie will go home in the trap with the biggest basket of grocery his mother has ever seen."

"That is good of you."

"Not at all."

"I don't really think it was your chauffeur's fault, you know."

"Heavens, of course not. We leave those children free of the woods but, my goodness, they run about as if they own them. It will teach the boy a lesson. Richard, I'm so glad you came early. I did want you to come for longer, you know."

"Yes, and I am grateful. But I have things to do in town."

"The Society. I know. I'm delighted. And I'm very glad you could manage the Wednesday. The others won't be here till Friday and until then you shall be my exclusive concern."

"Oh, please—"

"You have not been well. I owe it to your aunt. Portia is in the garden. Go and keep her company. I shall have some tea sent out to you."

"Thank you, Mrs Menant." He went to join Portia.

Three

"Hallo, Portia."

"Oh." She let her book close on one finger and glanced at him as ungraciously as she spoke. "It's you."

"Afraid so. May I?" He sat down. "What are you reading?"

She looked away from him, glum, and flipped a hand up toward him to show him the spine of the book.

"George Moore. What's it like?"

"Ditchwater."

"Why do you read it?"

"Bored."

"Oh."

"I'm always bored down here."

"Oh. Are you?"

"Well, I mean." She waved a hand at the country-side. He said nothing. She opened her book again, giving an impression of not taking it in but of seeking sanctuary from him.

The day was dazzling bright. The dark green glassy lake gave off a small local coolness but shot incandescent reflections of sunlight at him like bolts of fire. The scent of mowing from the lawn was heady. From among the back premises wheels rattled and voices prattled. Birds made their various small agreeable noises incessantly in the immense blue sky. Richard sat forward, elbows on the hot arms of his chair, fingers laced together. He was conscious of his bright red face and the tiny beads of sweat springing on his forehead. He must, he thought, be rather disgusting to a pretty girl. He wondered how to break the silence.

"It is peaceful, though."

"What?" Her quick, sulky look suggested that she had been torn away from the most spellbinding of stories.

"Here. It's ever so peaceful."

"Ha!" She applied herself to her book once more.

"I suppose, though—"

"What do you suppose?"

"Well, I can see why you prefer London."

"Can you? How perceptive!"

As became Richard's mentor in advanced views she wore a plain tan skirt and a white blouse with a small bow tie matching the skirt. Was she beautiful? Sometimes he thought so, sometimes the opposite. She was slim and taller than most girls, looking the more so because of her costume and her posture, which was habitually upright. Her hair was fairer than his, of a yellow as glossy and almost as bright as buttercup petals. It was done up in coils with a centre parting. Her skin was light, unaffected by the heat. Her grey eyes had never, at least in his presence, showed any warmth to anyone or about anything. And out of this face, whose expressions were seldom anything but pettish, scornful, bored or enigmatically blank, protruded a nose that was slightly too prominent at the nostrils, slightly too turned up at the tip. One could think of it, as he generally did, as saucy or delightful. Or one could see it coldly, as, alas, he sometimes did, as an absurd touch.

He searched his mind for words but he was in that

state he knew well when he was with Portia, in which not a word is to be found.

She was twenty-one, a year younger than he. She attended Ladies' Lectures at the Bedford College of London University without, as far as he knew, any particular objective in mind. During term she lived in the care of his Aunt Marian at the house in Bayswater; a very proper and kindly thing for his aunt to do for the daughter of a friend, and a most convenient arrangement. Not that there was much chaperonage involved. Portia came and went without saying much, although she frequently brought home clusters of girl friends and sometimes young men, usually after a curt announcement at short notice, as if Aunt Marian were a housekeeper. Aunt Marian thought Portia was a little hussy. Regrettably, so did a lot of other people.

He managed at last to say, "But you must miss the Society when you're down here?"

"Miss it? It bores me."

"But you've always been such an enthusiast."

"Am I?"

In truth it was hard to imagine Portia showing enthusiasm in any aspect of appearance or behaviour. He tried to think what he meant by enthusiasm : assiduity in going to Fabian Society meetings, in using its jargon to lecture other people – was that all? He said, "Aren't you?"

"I am interested in ideas. Theirs among others."

A maid came with the tea tray. Portia sat upright till the tray was on the table and the maid was titupping back to the house. She said, "How limiting to be a slave to one idea!"

"Oh, dear. And you made me a Fabian."

"I?"

"You did."

"I am not responsible for you."

"No – I suppose not."

"Also," she said, "it's a pretty dreadful crowd."

"But there are all sorts of brilliant people—"

"On the platform. Anyway, I get enough of them down here. But if you like sitting at meetings among a lot of horrid dowdy little women from the suburbs, and spotty young men who live in digs, I don't." She handed him his cup of tea.

"There has to be a rank-and-file."

"Of which you form one?"

"I am your recruit."

"And if I am bored with it, will you be, too?"

"No. I'm interested."

"Really? One wouldn't think so. I've never seen you get up to speak."

"Oh, I couldn't do that. But I like to listen. And I do try to help."

"I'm sure your envelope-addressing is invaluable. You're one of life's envelope-addressers, aren't you, Richard?"

"I'm afraid so."

Having sipped twice, she forgot her tea and returned to her book. Richard gave himself up to the peace of the morning, and tried to pick out one by one all the distant charming noises of live things, trains, human activity. It was a refuge.

Richard met Mr Menant that evening, in the drawing-room, before dinner. He saw at once who Portia took after in appearance. He had dozed on his bed all the afternoon, having been virtually driven to his room by Mrs Menant, who took seriously the notion that he must rest. She liked, it was clear, to think of herself as a person who commanded obedience, although it was not so much a natural air of authority to which Richard deferred as an unceasing nervy insistence which it was less fatiguing to humour than to resist.

He wondered during the afternoon where Portia was in the house, whether she had taken refuge from the baking heat or from his boring self.

At five-twenty he was startled out of a waking dream by the sound of the car arriving, the bang of the front door, a heavy tread and a deep male voice that ascended the stairs and dwindled to a muffled murmur in a first-floor room. That, he assumed, was Mr Menant. He had been informed at luncheon that Mr Menant went up to the City several times in each normal week, leaving by car at seven-forty-five in the morning to catch the train at Lewes and arriving home at seven in the evening. Today he had left London Bridge early, at two-thirty.

Mrs Menant had also enlarged upon her husband's business activities. It appeared that he was in the Africa trade. His father had made a great deal of money in West Africa, and had returned to London broken in health to run the business from an office in King William Street.

Ralph Menant had gone from Harrow into the business and had himself spent four years on the Gold Coast, miraculously without scathe. He had come home to marry and in the years that followed he had expanded the business into the southern reaches of Africa, just at

23

the right time, the late eighties and the nineties, amassing a moderate fortune. "He might have been a millionaire," Mrs Menant said in the high, taut voice of virtue, "if he had cared to ape those Jew gamblers on the Rand. But my husband has always said that if trade follows the flag – as it has, and why not? – it must also follow the precepts of decency."

Bathed and changed, Richard came down to the drawing-room a little before seven o'clock. His host was already there, in dinner jacket and black tie, lounging in a Knole settee. He put down his *Times* and rose to shake hands with Richard.

Mr Menant's hair must once have been as fair as his daughter's. Now it was tarnished by the passage of fifty-odd years, perhaps, too, by African suns, barbered in neat waves that showed agreeable streaks of grey. He had the same grey eyes as Portia and his was the nose on which hers had been modelled, standing out from a weather-battered face like a sundial pointer. With these physical features the resemblance ended for everything about him was easy and likeable. He was big, his face was broad and genial in structure as well as expression, his movements and lounging attitudes indicative of good humour. To Richard he looked more like the easygoing sort of schoolmaster than a City man.

"It was good of you to come," he said.

"Not at all."

"Company for Portia."

"I hope so."

"She does get bored on her own. Dessy – that's our younger girl – is staying down at Weymouth with Perdita, my oldest daughter, who is, as I expect you know, married."

24

"Yes. Portia has spoken of them both."

"And my wife spends a good deal of the day in seclusion. I'm sure you also know about her literary interests."

"Oh, yes. Aunt Marian shows me all her articles. About women's suffrage, and socialism, and all that."

"Indeed, and all that. You will notice that my girls are all Shakespearian heroines – Perdita, Portia and Desdemona. My wife is Hermione. My wife's mother was also a lady of some literary attainments. Hence the tradition. And how are you these days?"

"Oh, much better."

"Got over your illness, have you?"

"Yes. Yes, I should think so."

"Dreadful business that. You might have been murdered."

"Well, I wasn't. Not even concussed, really."

Richard did social work in the East End of London and lived intermittently at a social settlement. Last January on one of his errands about the slums he had been knocked down in a fog and robbed.

"I understood that there have been after-effects."

"Oh – some sort of shock, I suppose. It's wearing off."

But was it? And *what* was it? Richard wished people wouldn't ask him about his illness. He didn't feel ill, only troubled, greatly so. He hadn't talked about it. (Except once or twice to his doctor, on fruitless visits.) But Aunt Marian did and, unfortunately, so did everybody else who had heard of his misadventure.

"You were at Göttingen."

"Yes. Till last summer."

Richard's father had been a civil engineer in India. Both his parents had died of cholera when he was six.

He had been brought up since then by his aunt. He had some money of his own and the expectation of hers. She was unmarried. She had been good to him. He loved her. She had sent him to a public school and then, because she had once had a sweetheart in Germany, sent him to that country for his university years.

"What do you plan to do?"

"I don't know."

"You ought to fit yourself for something besides social work."

"I know. I was going to read law. But since that knock on the head I've—" He made a gesture of uncertainty.

"Of course. But you know, the best cure is to be doing something."

"I am doing something."

"Portia's Fabians?"

"And the settlement. Aunt Marian wonders how I could go there after what happened to me in Whitechapel, but lightning doesn't strike twice in the same place, does it? I take English classes."

"I am glad to hear that the labouring poor want English classes."

"It's mainly immigrants."

"Ah, yes. I suppose your unpaid work at the Fabian office is Portia's doing."

"Yes."

"I suppose all you young men do Portia's bidding."

"I should think so."

"I wonder why. She's a little horror."

Mrs Menant came in. She was wearing an evening gown of an iridescent blue with bead trimmings. They rose for her. Mr Menant said, "I'm glad you asked this young man down, my dear. We should have done so before. Marian has been very good to Portia."

"I think Portia might have asked him," said Mrs Menant, "but you know what that girl is."

Richard wondered if he would ever meet anyone who liked Portia.

"Are you and Portia good friends?" Mr Menant asked.

"Oh, yes. I mean— We don't see an awful lot of each other. I don't live at Aunt Marian's, you see, though I have a room there. I share a flat at the settlement with two other chaps."

"Of course. But you go to the Fabian meetings together."

"Oh, yes, and we walk in the Park and all that."

A clock struck the half-hour. Mr Menant said, "Portia is always last down. I sometimes think she sits up there calculating exactly the degree of annoyance she shall arouse before she descends." He turned to Richard. "About a career, my boy. Have you ever thought of commerce?"

"No. I'm not very good at figures."

"Everything can be learned if you have the willpower. And if you have that, you will soon be leaving the figures to subordinates."

"Oh," Richard said dubiously, "willpower."

"Would you like a try at it?"

"A try, sir?"

"I would start you in my office. Strictly at the bottom. No favours. As I would the son of any good friend."

"Oh—" It was a sound of consternation. "Thank you, sir."

"You might find it unexpectedly romantic."

"Yes. I do see what you mean, sir—" Richard's voice still sounded an unmistakable note of dismay.

"You don't by any chance look down on commerce?"

Mrs Menant cut in like a whip. "I should hope not." She looked at Richard as fiercely as if he had confessed that he did. "My husband is a man of wide cultivation. He has political interests—"

"Not the same as yours, my dear. Though I am always open —" he addressed this to Richard – "to ideas, and I keep my house open to them."

"Ralph, I wish you would not interrupt me."

"My dear, I am humbly sorry."

"My husband," she said to Richard, "is also a considerable landowner. Men like him have as great a stake in the country as any. The mercantile spirit has produced in the last fifty years some of our finest intellects and some of our greatest exemplars of philanthropy and, what is more important, social conscience. Think of the Booths and families like them. Men like my husband are coming to the fore in every sphere. I see no merit in blue blood, nor much in those who claim to be the only true gentry, as they term it. Gentry. We may not be of such gentry, but we are gentlefolk, and so are you, Richard. And you should be honoured at the chance to follow in my husband's footsteps."

"Oh," said Richard, "I am. Truly. Only—"

"You want time, that is all," said Mr Menant. "Digest it. There's no hurry. But don't be too shy to come and talk about it whenever you want to."

"Oh, no," said Richard. "Thank you, sir."

"I shall tell Hawker to serve dinner," said Mrs Menant.

"Don't do that," her husband said.

"Then I shall send a maid to Portia. I will not have my family coming and going to and from table as they please."

Portia came in and caused another tic of displeasure in her mother's face, for she had changed into nothing more formal than a high-necked lace blouse, which she wore with a jacket and skirt in brown and beige stripes. She had, however, done something to her hair that made this one of the times when Richard thought her beautiful. She said, "I'm starving. Aren't you ever going in to dinner?"

Thursday night was bright and moonlit. At one a.m. Richard was walking on the east lawn. His second day had been, as days went, a good day. He had walked on Long Down in the morning with Portia. He had been fed at every mealtime with cream and honey and all manner of tasty things by her mother, who might have been secluded most of the day in the study writing about suffrage and socialism, but who found time to keep at the heels of cook and maids and manservant and gardeners and to ensure that the fare on her table was of the best. He had slept after luncheon and had afternoon tea by the lake with Portia. True, she had been sulky on the walk, pacing ahead of him, kicking the turf and frowning as if she had troubles which were entirely private but for which, mysteriously, she blamed him; and when he had tried, in blurts of talk, to draw her out at tea-time she had answered in few syllables and maintained, mostly, a moody silence.

But he was used to this. She had never been otherwise to him. He was terribly in love with her. There was nothing moony or sloppy about it; he did not feel he resembled the comic swains in *Punch*. It was like vitriol dashed at his insides whenever he saw her. Sometimes he felt as if he were going mad, congested to bursting at the temples. At their first meeting, at his aunt's last year, when he returned from Germany, he had hardly noticed her except as a silly, spoilt girl. The second time and ever since he had felt like this.

As often as not when he went to his aunt's, Portia was there. She always greeted him in the same colourless voice, with the same indifferent glance. He went with her to Fabian meetings. Sometimes he prevailed upon her to walk with him in Hyde Park or to go with him to a concert. She went, but she was remote from him all the time, lacklustre. Occasionally she was rude to him, in a dull, uncaring way. This was less painful to him than her consistent uninterestedness. He had accepted her mother's invitation knowing that to be in the same house as Portia for six days would be torture, but he came like an iron filing to a magnet.

At twenty-two he was virgin. He wanted girls and there had been pleasant, inviting *mädels* in Germany, but their encouragements had not been enough to overcome his shyness. His own failure to respond had destroyed the little confidence he had.

Desire was a frequent torment but it did not drive him to even the most inoffensive attack upon Portia's indifference. Her presence numbed desire as it numbed his tongue. Yet lurking in him was some hope, some fiction which in another part of himself he knew to be delusive, that this weekend might in some unforeseeable way create the conditions for a change in her – a sudden warm smile, a glance even that took notice of him, a revelation (now his mind soared into fantasy) that her rejection had only been a mask behind which she had all the time after her own mysterious fashion cared for him. Oh, he didn't know what he thought or hoped for. A will-o'-the-wisp led him on.

Portia was awake and saw him from her window, which was on the main floor above the east lawn. She knew that he suffered. She had known from their earliest meetings. She felt an impulse of pleasure that he was walking down there, to and fro beneath her window. She, too, had a secret life, and in it young men did this sort of thing. She went to bed feeling a kind of affection towards Richard, and slept well.

Richard knew that he was walking beneath her window and it added a touch to his general melancholy. But he was not walking on the lawn, awake at one a.m., because of Portia.

He had put on dressing-gown and slippers over his striped pyjamas and found his way out of the house by a small side door, sweating and scared. He had had one of his dreams. But was it a dream? He had seen what he had seen lying in bed, wide awake, his eyes open. It was a dream (if it was a dream) that he had had six weeks before. For the second time he had seen the death of his Aunt Marian.

Four

At dinner on Thursday evening, and afterwards, Mrs
Menant was visibly nervous. Her ill-temper at Portia's
lateness was only a symptom. The cause, Richard soon
realised, was F. J. Dobbs, the novelist. She said, "I
wonder if I should have sent him a telegram today."

Mr Menant said, "What on earth for?"

"To get him to confirm."

"Of course he'll come."

She said, in a fretting tone that exposed her anxiety,
"I suppose he will."

Portia went on eating her lamb without appearing
to hear anything.

A little later Mrs Menant said, "I've moved the
Perugino triptych to the West Bedroom. And the Burne-
Jones drawings. I hope he likes it."

"A bit overpowering for a bedroom," her husband
said.

"I tried hanging the Flemish tapestry in there but it
looked rather shabby. The sunlight catches it."

"My dear," Mr Menant said, "he has simple tastes.
He doesn't want an art gallery. Only a bedroom. And
it is our best."

"He has no reason to look down on it," she said,
defiantly, as if already answering a complaint from the
guest. "Mr Shaw has slept in it."

• •

"Don't talk to me about Mr Shaw. I feel guilty now every time I eat a chop."

Later, in the drawing-room, Mrs Menant said, "I wonder if I should have written to his wife."

"Whyever should you have done that? She never goes with him."

"I know that. Perhaps I should have asked about his likes and dislikes."

Portia was turning over the pages of a magazine. Richard was trying to maintain in a facial expression that had put him under more and more strain all the evening, the right blend of earnest attention to a hostess and polite detachment from private family argument.

"My dear, you managed Shaw. After that you should have no more worries."

"I cannot help it if I take my responsibilities seriously."

Portia looked up and said, "Why is he coming? After all, we are nobodies."

"Portia, don't be ridiculous," her mother said. "Mr Dobbs wrote to me most appreciatively when I sent him a copy of my last novel."

"I dare say he does to everybody."

"You only know how to depreciate, my girl. He was extremely nice to us at the Webbs' *soirée* in June. He spoke most earnestly to your father for a long time."

"Cadging Stock Exchange tips, I suppose."

Ralph Menant leaned back in his chair, quietly chuckling, smiling with eyes closed.

"I don't think a girl's rudeness is amusing, Ralph," his wife said.

"But she is right, my dear," he said. "She is precisely right." He gave himself up to another few seconds of chuckling. "Dobbs really is an atrocious cad. The sort of fellow who wears a boater at Margate and plays the banjo."

"He is a great man."

"That, too, perhaps. My dear, you may be sure your socialist idol will come. He made a packet out of the last tip I gave him."

On Friday morning, to escape the ordeal of meeting a succession of guests as they arrived, Richard begged some sandwiches from his hostess and went for a long walk. He was always in an anguish before meeting new people, especially such a pride of lions as he imagined Mrs Menant's guests to be. He foresaw himself looking ridiculous (and looking so before Portia) either by silence or by blurting out silly things in a vain effort to take part.

He came back at three in the afternoon, hoping to sneak in through the orchard behind the house, then through a back door to his room. A bath, change and rest till dinner would delay the ordeal.

A tall, clipped yew hedge separated the gardens from the orchard. A small wrought-iron gate in the hedge enabled him to enter the garden, on the south side of the lake. There were two large lawns here, one for croquet. He started across the other, which led to the house.

"Hallo, there!"

He stopped and turned, and felt the familiar skip of panic in his breast. A man stood only a dozen feet from him, alone; bent over a croquet mallet, about to knock a ball through a hoop. "Hallo, there," the man said again, "who are you?"

Richard had recognised, as would have any even semi-

34

literate person in the country, F. J. Dobbs. His throat was too parched with shyness for him to speak.

"Come on, old chap," F.J. smiled. He was a smaller man than Richard had imagined. "I don't eat people. You know my name, don't you?"

"Yes, sir." It was the smile that thawed Richard, the most reassuring that he could for years remember seeing; and something in the eyes, a mild, tentative scrutiny, and, somehow, the accent, ever so slightly tinged with – might it have been the country sound or the Cockney sound or both? "Oh, yes, sir. I'm Richard Latt. How do you do, sir?"

"How de do." They shook hands. "You look hot."

"Yes, sir." Richard had gone walking in whites. He was dismally conscious of grass stains on his trousers and (for it was another blazing day) his shirt sagging on his back, cold and wet with sweat which showed in great dark patches. He had his jacket over his shoulders, a finger still hooked through the hanging-tab. "I've been walking."

"Come along—" A table and chair had been set out for F.J. On the table were a jug and glass. "Have some lemonade. I'm a common sort of chap. I don't mind sharing my glass."

"Thank you, sir. May I?"

"And sit down, while you're about it." F.J. leaned the mallet against the hedge and sat down with Richard. "Where did you walk?"

"Up on the Downs towards Lewes. I didn't go right in. I swung round and came back above Firle."

"Good walking, that. I like the Downs. That springy feeling under your feet, eh?"

"Yes, sir."

"Larks trilling and tumbling, eh? And the silence?"

F.J. had hung the jacket of his dark grey suit on the back of a chair, exposing his braces without shame. He wore a white shirt with a soft, open collar. His face was as familiar to Richard as Aunt Marian's. A score of cartoonists had made it so, and Richard saw it as precisely the sum of those characteristics so often scored by the thick black pencils of caricature : pudgy cheeks, bags under the eyes, Cockney-clerk's fringe of greying bronze hair on his forehead, thick eyebrows and thick ragged moustache drooping over a small mouth.

The conversation lagged for a moment and Richard, who had been wondering in discomfort whether he had a duty to perform, began, "Sir, I – er—"

He fell silent.

"Yes?"

"I've— Mr Dobbs, I've read all your books. I've— I expect everybody tells you about admiring them and all that."

F.J. leaned an elbow on the table, chewed the thumb of that hand, and managed at the same time to indulge in scarcely audible inward laughter.

"I'm sorry, sir. I didn't know whether I ought. I mean—"

F.J. let the arm on which he was leaning cant forward across the table so that he leaned with it. "My lad, it bloody irritates me."

"Oh, I see."

"I can't meet a soul without having to endure a prologue either of gush or of gormless stammer. On the other hand, I suppose I'd be rather furious if I didn't get it."

36

Richard remained silent and tried to look understanding.

"You see," said F.J., "writers are conceited. There are modest ones, but their conceit is secret, and it devours them. A writer couldn't go on without conceit. He has to bury his lack of self-confidence as deep as possible."

"Yes, sir."

"And tell me, Richard Latt, are you a friend of the family?"

"Yes, sir. In a way. My Aunt Marian Holland is a lifelong friend of Mrs Menant."

"Ah. Been down here before?"

"No, sir. I came for the first time on Wednesday."

"Aha. Do you like your food?"

"My food, sir?"

"Are you a good eater?"

"Oh, yes, sir."

"And?"

"And? Oh – yes, yes, Mrs Menant keeps an absolutely splendid table."

"Ah." F.J. settled back contentedly.

Richard felt it was his turn to keep the conversation going. From some depth in his suddenly-emptied mind he dredged up, dreading that it was the wrong thing but unable not to utter it, "Sir, are you, er – are you writing another book?"

"Yes. And let's leave it at that."

"Oh." Of course he was doomed, always, to say the wrong thing. "I *am* sorry."

"Not a question to press. Not with me. Horrid. And think yourself lucky I'm not the other sort of writer."

"The other sort?"

"The sort who would pin you down for the rest of

the afternoon telling you all about it. I say, I hate sitting still, don't you? Come and knock a croquet ball about."

"I— I am rather a mess, sir. I really ought to bathe and change. Suppose the ladies came out?"

"Ah," F.J. said, "the ladies. Sweat is as likely to excite as to sicken them."

Richard was looking straight at F.J. in bewilderment. F.J. smiled, and Richard was stirred deeply by something, after all, that was exceptional in the man, in his eyes. There was the never-ceasing scrutiny. It seemed to be not only of Richard's outward person but of things inside him and beyond him; and it was of such mildness and directness that it did not upset him. There were flitting intimations of compassion and an odd quality of sadness. F. J. said, "Tell me more about yourself, Richard Latt."

"I was in Germany for three years. At Göttingen. I came back last autumn."

"Doing what?"

"Philosophy."

"Of course. What else? You know it was a waste of time?"

"No, sir."

"Classical philosophy is tosh. Medieval philosophy is worse. And German philosophy is the dregs of idiocy, to which no doubt you were thoroughly subjected. Teutonic system-mongering."

"I see, sir. In that case, I—"

"Well?"

"It all went in at one ear and out at the other. You've cheered me up no end, sir."

F.J. laughed and Richard, relaxing wonderfully,

laughed with him; and took heart so that he heard himself blurt, "I'm not really such an ass, sir."

"No?"

"I just read for the whole three years, sir. I just read and read and read."

"What?"

"Everything, sir."

"Except philosophy."

"Afraid so. I've read all the modern novelists, sir, and Ibsen and Shaw."

"And you've read me?"

"Oh, I just pounced on your books, sir. I couldn't wait to get them." Richard marvelled that words came so easily to him. F.J. was settled in his chair, basking, as it seemed, in the sunshine.

"Pray go on, Richard Latt."

"You're so exciting, sir. I don't think anybody can be young and not be excited by your work."

"Yes," F.J. said, "the young. They're the ones I want to hear from. They don't irritate me. My novels, I suppose you mean."

"And your essays. I got *Looking Forward* when it came out in May. My head just span with new ideas. And I went to both your lectures at the Fabian this year."

"Socialist, are you?"

"I don't know, sir."

"You don't know? Hermione Menant told me you worked at the Fabian office."

"Yes, sir. But – you see, I just go along and listen."

"Listen? You don't think? You don't come back with ideas of your own?"

"Oh, yes, sir. I do. I do have ideas. But you see, I

39

read something or hear something, and it seems so indisputable, so *tremendous* – only when I think about it afterwards I see all sorts of qualifying factors – and questions I'd like to ask."

"Do you ask the questions?"

"No, sir."

"Why not?"

Richard remained quiet. F.J. said, "All right, Richard Latt. I know. Let me tell you something. Until I was twenty everyone called me a dull boy. People talked all round me and I just sat there with a fish face and no doubt a gaping mouth. A little village idiot. I couldn't get words out. But there was a tumult inside my head."

Richard was so grateful that he felt tears inside his eyelids. He could only say, a little hoarsely, "Yes, sir."

F.J. waited, his gentle smile upon Richard; and Richard, astonished, heard words tumbling out of himself. "I can't tell you, sir. I feel as if I'm trying to take in the whole world and my head's not big enough. You know, I think about things, and inside my head, well, I feel I'm being frightfully clever, but—"

F.J. said, "Yes."

And Richard sat, astonished, translated into happiness.

"People call me F.J. I'm not fond of that 'sir'. Makes me sound old. I'm not. I'm forty-one." He jumped up.

"And what's more Richard Latt, I hope you're not a slacker."

"Slacker – F.J.?"

"I hate spending a weekend with slackers loafing around in chairs. I like games, exercise, doing things, getting up things."

"Oh, yes, yes. It could be great fun."

"I shall count on you, Richard Latt. Lots of go. Everything Jolly. Friends, eh?"

"Oh – oh, yes, F.J."

In a daze, Richard felt his hand being shaken again. A friendship sealed, with, of all men, this one.

"My word," F.J. said, "you are in a sweat. Cut along and have your bath."

Richard cried, "Oh, yes, sir," and, like a child, broke into an exultant run on his way back to the house.

The other guests did not seem half so formidable as before to Richard now that he felt himself, as it were, under F.J.'s wing. Henry Redington, a senior Civil Servant at the Treasury, came with his wife Jane. The pair of them had made a reputation as sociologists. Miss Snell, who had founded a famous ladies' college and worked for women's rights, was athletic, elderly and to Richard unexpectedly beautiful with her girl's complexion and shining white hair. In the drawing-room before dinner she heartened him by speaking to him most kindly.

The last arrival was Mr Argent, the Labour leader. He was a tall, courtly man, with silver hair romantically waved and a tiny, timorous wife. They were spending the summer at Seaford where Mr Argent was convalescing after a heart attack, forbidden by his doctors, as he repeatedly and eloquently explained, to attend the House of Commons in spite of all the exciting events that were just now taking place in that assembly.

At dinner Richard was two places from F.J., who sat in the position of honour at Mrs Menant's left, but he was comforted by the great man's presence. There was a greater reason for his being happy tonight. A

Portia transformed sat across the table. She, who in his company had always appeared in the simple, severe dress of the young New Woman, had struck him into a trance of delight when she walked, all the more conspicuous for being as usual late, into the drawing-room.

Her dress was a sheath of pale gold cut severely straight from shoulder to toe, almost matching her hair and making her look like a slender golden figurine. The dress had wide straight sleeves and was not marred by any ornament. Richard gazed at her over a bowl of roses and wondered.

The dining-room was simple but splendid, its walls panelled in painted Spanish leather, its old floorboards brought to a gleaming polish. The table was splendid with napery, silver, roses chosen and arranged by their hostess and crystal glasses. The meal was splendid, too, which made Richard happy, because he felt that he had given a guarantee on the subject to F. J. Maids came and went quietly, and served deftly, their caps and aprons crisp and snowy. Hawker was aloof in the background, directing them. Mrs Menant, at the head of the table, was content with her achievement and looked for once in repose.

Mrs Menant said, "I hope there will be no formality this weekend. You must all relax and rest from your labours."

Mousy little Mrs Argent squeaked, "Oh, thank you," and F.J. said, "Rest for the tired warrior, eh?"

"We are all warriors, in the cause of good," Mr Argent intoned.

Redington said, "My dear Hermione, if I were at home, I should be dining in a velvet jacket and a soft collar and tie, and not in this absurd penguin uniform that convention requires."

"Ah," said Mr Argent, "a Bohemian."

Miss Snell said, "Surely it is no more than a mark of courtesy."

Mr Redington : "To whom ?"

"To one's companions."

Mr Menant spoke from his end of the table. "Surely it's just a matter of getting out of one's working rags each day and into something decent."

Richard took in the words but his mind was on Portia. She was so changed. It was not just the dress, it was her whole air. She looked so soft, so relaxed. There was a grace in her movements he had not discerned before. He had never seen her look so gentle, yet so exciting to his senses. She sat and listened to the table talk with a demureness he would never have expected in her, hardly touching her wine; of which, as was proper with an unmarried girl, she had only been served a token drop.

Mr Argent's famous voice was as silvery as his hair. "There are certain forms which are of positive social value. One might call them indices of civilisation. We do not strive to abolish such forms but to place them within the reach of all."

"Exactly," Mrs Menant said. "Within the reach of all. That is what one strives for."

F.J. looked up from his plate. He said, "Cor blimey."

Everyone looked at the lion. But he resumed his own pleasant, slightly common accent. "I take the most vulgar pleasure in putting on evening dress. It's the badge of what I've achieved. Don't under-estimate the

43

satisfaction of getting on in the world. Eh, Argent? You've got on."

"I do agree," said Mr Argent, "that there must be symbols of achievement, hierarchical symbols if you will, to encourage people to endeavour. One might see them as the ladder by which the people will ascend to socialism."

"Do you mean," Mr Menant put in, "that the nearer we come to socialism, the more of our workpeople will dress for dinner?"

Everybody laughed except Richard and Portia; for Richard dared to offer Portia across the table a tentative smile which had nothing to do with Mr Menant's witticism; and she once again astonished him by responding with a small, quick smile before redirecting a respectful gaze at F.J.

"Ah," said F.J., "the whole point of achievement is that only a few ever achieve."

Mrs Menant, in triumph, "Exactly."

"Most work will always be mean and mind-destroying," F.J. said, "and regrettably, though perhaps fortunately for us, Nature has seen to it that most of the species is capable of no mental effort greater than that which is commensurate with, let us say, sticking labels on jamjars."

"But we must do what we can for them," Mr Argent said.

"Melioration," said Redington. "Remorseless melioration."

"But when all is said and done," announced Mrs Menant, "one does not have to wear evening dress to stick labels on jamjars."

Polite laughter for the hostess.

"To a poor old-fashioned Liberal like me," Mr Menant said, "you present socialism as the great aristocratic creed of our time."

"And why not?" F.J.'s voice became squeaky when he raised it, but it had a merry, challenging effect. "*Elites* are emerging which can lead mankind to the promised land – the scientists, the great creative industrialists – the airmen. Think of the unprecedented power of yea or nay that each of these will command. The problem of the future will be to establish the new orders of aristocracy."

Richard was at ease. He was happy to be at this table, listening to this talk. He was happy, too, at Portia's modest demeanour. He felt that in this new self she displayed there was some hope for him.

She was the same, later on, in the drawing-room. The men joined the ladies and Richard saw her curled in a low armchair by the window. She remained there outside the main group, listening in silence to the conversation, as unregarded by all the other guests, it seemed to Richard, as a cat in the room might be.

The talk was inevitably of the storms that were raging in Parliament. "A vote of confidence on Monday," Mr Argent lamented, "and I may not be there. I wished to go. I determined to go, if it cost my life—"

A weak little, "Oh, no!" from his wife.

"—but the doctor has most positively forbidden it. After all, my life is not my own to dispose of. I think I may say the nation needs it."

Mrs Menant cried, "Hear, hear."

F.J. said, "The House can spare you. It's only shadowboxing. There'll be a hundred majority for the Government. The Bill's as good as through."

45

He was referring to the Liberal Government's Parliament Bill, which deprived the House of Lords of most of its obstructive powers and which the Lords had thrown out. The Government had retaliated by threatening to create a mass of new Liberal peers who would vote the Bill through. In face of this the Lords and the Conservatives were in a turmoil of angry demonstrations but there had, indeed, been intimations in the last week that they would back down.

Redington said, "I hear the French are backing down, too."

Quickly, to show that she knew what he was talking about, Mrs Menant cried, "Agadir?"

"It looked an ugly business for a time," Redington said. "We had to warn the Germans that we'd come in if there was war with France. Did you know that our Fleet is still coaling? We have to show we mean business with the German Grand Fleet at sea."

"Surely—" Mrs Menant began.

"No, no, no," Redington assured her. "It won't come to war."

The Germans had sent a cruiser to the coast of Morocco under the pretext of protecting their nationals; and had enlarged the dispute with France into a demand for part of the French colonies in Africa.

Mr Menant said, "Berlin and Paris have agreed on fundamentals. The French will give some of their Congo territories to Wilhelm. There'll probably be an international conference to settle the details. It's in today's *Times*."

"There you are!" Mrs Menant spoke as if she had had a hand in the settlement.

"Give and take," her husband said. "It's the only way."

"Arbitration." This was Mr Argent, in his platform voice. "The age of brute force is over. The era of arbitration has begun. Is it not fitting that President Taft is the torchbearer, with his Arbitration Treaties? The great new democracy across the sea heralding the great new age?—"

"Indeed," his host said, unable to conceal the faintest falling note of weariness; and, perhaps because Mr Argent seemed about to resume, Miss Snell reached out to touch a silver bowl on a table next to her. "What beautiful filigree work!"

F.J. said, "That's a pretty piece," and started to heave himself up out of his chair.

For the first time since dinner Portia spoke. "Don't get up, Mr Dobbs."

Richard, whose every nerve was strained to her, was startled by her voice suddenly raised and by the way she glided quickly across the room with the bowl. Again he was puzzled by that something new and disturbing in her appearance and her movements. She stood in front of F.J. holding the bowl out in both hands.

"Ah—" F.J. looked at the bowl, turned it with his finger, looked up at her. She looked down to meet his eyes, her gaze, to the watching Richard, indifferent as ever.

F.J. said, "Thank you."

She took the bowl back to her corner and sat down.

Richard let the conversation flow on, half-listening while he wondered what Portia's smile to him at dinner could have meant.

47

Of course it drifted back to politics. Redington said, "I hear you had Asquith down here."

Mrs Menant said, "He did us the honour to stop here for luncheon during his tour of Sussex constituencies."

"Are you going to stand for Parliament?" Redington asked Ralph Menant.

"My dear chap," Menant said, "I'm too old to start in that game."

"Then what is the nature of your interest in the Liberal Party?"

"Just that of a sympathetic spectator."

Portia broke her silence again. "My father would like to be made a baronet. He wants to set up as a squire and look the landed gentry in the face. Though Heaven knows why, he hasn't got any sons."

The subsequent moment of silence was broken by F.J. He said to Mrs Menant, "I hope for the sake of Asquith's digestion you didn't talk to him about women's suffrage when he was here."

"Not a word."

"She made a gallant effort for my sake," Ralph Menant said.

F.J. looked across the room. "And you, Miss Menant?"

"I was banished," Portia said. "I wasn't allowed down that day on pain of death."

Miss Snell said, "Mr Asquith is the arch-enemy of all women's aspirations. He has twice ignored the will of Parliament that we be given the vote."

F.J. still looked at Portia. "And if you had been here, would you have given him a piece of your mind?"

Portia said, "I would have shot him."

F.J. kept his somewhat bulging eyes upon her, and in a mournful, dismissive voice said, "Ah."

"If anyone should be shot," Mr Menant said, "it is that scoundrel Lloyd George."

"Come," said Mr Argent, "you are surely not opposed to the National Insurance Bill?"

"I am opposed to Lloyd George. He is a menace to the Liberal Party and to the country."

"Because he wishes – and in this he has the support of Labour – to offer some small relief to the unemployed and to the sick poor?"

"Because he is a mob demagogue of the worst type."

"The Bill doesn't go very far," Redington said.

Ralph Menant said, "You spoke before of a new age. Lloyd George has offered the working man ninepence for fourpence. That is his slogan. Those very words. This is indeed the start of a new age. An age of bribery. The franchise will be extended and politics will become an auction, each party outdoing the other in irresponsible and ruinous bribes offered to the voters, the all-powerful mob."

"He may be all that you say," said Redington, "but he is compelled – the more of a demagogue, the more he is compelled – to contribute with his pension and insurance schemes to the inevitable process of betterment."

"Remorseless melioration," his wife said.

Mr Menant answered, "We are all in agreement that the lot of the poor must be bettered. But will you really condemn me as a heartless diehard if I suggest that the process must have its limits?"

"What limits?" Mrs Menant cried.

"The limit at which degrading want has been relieved."

Mr Argent said, "But why stop there? We aspire to far more."

F.J. sat slumped in his chair, listening like an adjudicator.

"One must stop at the point at which people must do the rest for themselves, having been given the opportunity to do so, the worst handicaps of poverty and ignorance removed. Otherwise the State simply gives and the mob takes. As in imperial Rome. Bread and Circuses. Politicians compete with bribes for the votes of the ignorant, encouraging people to believe that you can have ninepence for fourpence, which is impossible. The will to work and the will to self-defence become atrophied. Decline and fall."

Miss Snell spoke vigorously. "Never. You forget that men and women will change for the better as we change material conditions. That is what we educators work for."

"We fit the people," Mr Argent said, "to be worthy of higher things."

Redington said, "You forget that this time there are no barbarians at the frontiers."

His wife added, "None that can withstand the civilised countries."

Mr Menant said, "I speak in a commercial sense. There are no barbarians of any consequence – we may leave the Yellow Peril to the gutter Press – but there are trade rivals who are keen and efficient. And markets that may not always be our province."

F.J. sat forward. Everyone in the room waited for his opinion. But he spoke to Richard. "And what do you think, Richard Latt?"

Richard's heart thumped, with fright at being forced to speak, with joy at being honoured by F.J.'s particular attention. "Oh— Well, sir, we are all made in God's image. We must act so, and we must treat other people as if they are."

Mr Argent said, "Bravo! What greater command can there be to strive ever upward than Our Lord's?"

F.J. addressed himself again to Richard. "You are religious?"

"Oh, no, sir—F.J." It took him a moment to check his breathing and sort words out of his confusion. "I mean, yes, I do, sort of, believe – well, I go to church."

F.J. looked across to Portia. "And you, young woman?"

She remained curled up in her golden sheath, deep in the chair, looking back at him neutrally. "Me?"

"You. Sit up and don't pretend."

"Pretend what?"

"Pretend you're not interested. Are you a Christian?"

"No, Mr Dobbs."

"Why not?" Mr Argent's voice was benign. "I am able to reconcile science, progress and socialism with Christianity."

And like a thump across Richard's face, the old Portia spoke. "More fool you."

A second of total silence. Then F.J. laughed, a loud, lengthy, squeaky, joyful cachinnation to which he surrendered himself, leaning back in his chair. Portia appeared to have retreated into herself again, her face calm. Then F.J. sat up again. "I say, what about games this weekend?"

"There's the cricket on Monday," Ralph Menant said.

"I say, Richard, cricket!" F.J. seemed to have a child's power of total, glorious enjoyment. Richard saw and loved it in his big, comic smile, in the radiant merriment of his eyes. "Nothing like cricket, glorious game."

"We play the village. They field a rough lot but it's fun," Mr Menant said. "Most of our side will come from the estate, but I trust I can count on you two to join me in the team."

Richard cried, "Oh, rather!"

"I shan't ask you, Redington," Mr Menant said.

"You had better not."

"I say, Menant," F.J. said, "what about tennis? You keep your court in trim, I see."

"It's at your disposal."

"Who plays?"

"I do, rather well," Miss Snell said.

Richard, like a child inviting teacher's attention, "I do."

F.J. said, "And you, Miss Menant? Will you play?"

Portia said indifferently, "All right."

Nobody fawned on the lion of the weekend; the other guests were all too much of a world in which he was often, in one way or another, encountered. But when F.J. rose, in a mere pause in what appeared to be mid-conversation, and said shortly, "I'm for an early night. If you'll excuse me, Mrs Menant," the party broke up.

Richard bade his goodnights and went upstairs. F.J. had just reached the door of his room when Richard came on to the big landing, with the guest and family bedrooms and study around it. Richard said, "Goodnight, F.J.," but before he could disappear through the little door in the wall the writer checked him with a hand underneath the elbow. "Just a moment, Richard Latt—"

Portia came up and walked past them with a "Goodnight, Mr Dobbs," not looking round.

"Goodnight, Miss Menant." F.J.'s head was turned to see her go into her room, still not looking back at them. He said, "Cheeky bit. No corsets. Makes a difference, eh?"

The words made a flash in Richard's mind. But F.J. reclaimed his attention. "You see, my lad, you can use your tongue when you want to."

"Oh," Richard said. "I didn't much."

"You must practise more."

"Yes," said Richard, unhappy at the thought but also emboldened at being under such tutelage. "I will. Goodnight."

But F.J. detained him again. "I'll give you a cure for shyness. Do one outrageous thing – one really audacious thing every day."

Richard could only echo, on an expiring breath, "Audacious?"

"Something the very prospect of which makes you faint. It will be agony at first."

"I think it would."

"It will get easier."

"I'm afraid it wouldn't."

"Do it once. Once. And see. D'you hear me?"

"Yes."

"Goodnight, my boy."

F.J. went into the West Bedroom.

Richard turned off the light and opened the window. A light breeze and the scent of grass came in to him. The sky was bright with pale moonlight. Long Down was a black sleeping monster. A shaft of light shot out into the kitchen courtyard. A door opened and a woman came out to stand in the yard for a few moments, mysteriously still. Then she called, "Tibby, Tibby, Tibby." She went in. The door closed and the shaft of light went out. A few seconds later a white cat stole out of the open, yawning front of the dark garage, leaped on to a wall and stalked sinuously away. It all enchanted him. He stood at the window in a vague triumphant reverie.

No corsets. The knowingness of older men, perhaps of all other men! He would never have known. That was why she was so different, why she walked as softly and sinuously as that cat, why the subtle lines of her body moulded and moved that wonderful golden dress. Something about her had played upon his body and soul and he had not known what it was, only the delicious shiver of sensation through himself. She was a soft rounded thing, a woman, a body, flesh.

He lay down on his bed. Even with the breeze exploring the room it was too hot for coverings. Portia slept on the floor below. Her room was not directly beneath his but it made a convenient fantasy to imagine that it was, and that she lay there on her bed, unclad, slender, white.

Desire took hold of him. He got up. He would not degrade himself. He must not dirty his exquisite vision. He sluiced himself at the basin in cold water and went back to the window. He drifted into a reverie. It was of Portia, fresh, cool, untroubled by the heat of the night, sleeping like a white recumbent statue whose breast rose and fell by magic. Richard knew all about the mechanical workings of love, and they seemed a sweaty, lowering business to him now. That sort of thing did not interest his beautiful Portia. After all, young men came to hang about her at Aunt Marian's, but there was none in whom she showed any interest, no other than Richard with whom she ever bothered to go out.

His reverie became a story as usual. They married. He had courted her with chivalry. To her wonderment and joy he had told her what she had been waiting without hope for a man to tell her: that he wanted nothing from her but to be near him and let him serve her. Now on the wedding night he would not touch her. There she lies in her bed, looking up from a dainty pillow edged in frothy lace, one hand holding the sheet rumpled at her waist but afraid to pull it up to her chin for fear of making a crude, frightened gesture of refusal. But he stoops, kisses her brow reverently and retreats to sleep elsewhere, conscious of her smile of gratitude and her murmured, "Goodnight, darling." He comes again the next night, stoops to kiss her, and meets the deep, direct gaze of her eyes. He is about to straighten up, to turn away, but her white arms come up, her hands clasp behind his neck, she draws him down to her—

A word drifted across the front of his mind. Audacious. His attention darted after it. He stood at the window, whispering inside his mouth "l'audace, l'audace." New reveries grew around these words. A small inner disturbance of mirth shook his chest. He returned to his bed and soon he was asleep.

Five

There was no escape from F.J.'s jolliness. Next morning he dominated breakfast like a squeaky, bouncy games master, determined to protect his flock from the perils of idleness by everlastingly getting things up.

Richard roamed along the sideboard, in good appetite after his night's sleep. The row of immense, domed servers offered him fried eggs, heaps of bacon, chops, smoked haddock, trout and kedgeree, and there was a ham on a stand. He took two eggs and six rashers of bacon and sat down courageously (was he not F.J.'s pupil, the sorcerer's apprentice?) next to Portia. She was eating a slice of toast with marmalade.

Argent and his wife, Redington, and Mr Menant were down, all of them at table except Redington, who was backed against the sideboard with F.J.'s hands on his shoulders, engaged with F.J. in a duet of soprano urging and tenor expostulation. The question at issue was whether Redington would, after all, make a fourth at tennis.

Meanwhile, "Hallo, Portia," Richard said.

Portia said gloomily, "Hallo."

A moment of silence. Richard, brightly, "It looks like another beautiful day."

"Does it?"

"Yes."

"I suppose he's got you for tennis," she said.

"F. J. ?"

"Dreadful man."

"Oh." Then Richard decided to stand up for his idol. "I think he's an awfully nice fellow."

"Do you?"

"He can't help – well, you know, his mother was a housemaid or something."

"I suppose that's why he capers about like the jolly blacksmith."

"He's only trying to – well, I mean, he is immensely clever."

"Fat little bore. I suppose Mother has to get these big pots down. Meat and drink to her. Awful."

"I should have thought—"

"What should you have thought?"

"I should have thought it would be jolly interesting having all sorts of famous people coming down."

"Improving, I suppose. You are ghastly."

"Why?"

"Earnest."

"No, I'm not."

"Yes you are. All those walks in London. All you do is talk at me – earnestly."

"Oh. I am sorry. I thought you liked it."

"Does it seem so?"

"Sorry." A pause, painful to him. "Would you like some more toast?"

"No, thank you."

Miss Snell came in, "Good morning, everybody."

Her voice was clear, calm and strong. She spoke as if from the platform of her college hall to an assembly of her maidens. "I have not," she announced, "lain abed, although you must forgive my tardiness. I have been for a long walk over the Downs."

F.J. relinquished his prey, who forked a pair of trout on to his plate and went to the table. "Miss Snell," he said, "they told me you had gone out. I thought you had deserted us."

"You should have faith," she replied. "I volunteered last night, did I not?"

"You did. And so we have our four."

Portia made a most expressive grimace of unenthusiasm, turning to Richard but well aware that she was generally observed. "And I know," F.J. said, "that Miss Menant simply cannot wait."

Miss Snell proposed a mixed doubles.

"Oh, no," said F.J., "we must have a tournament. I do so adore winning, you know."

He wrote names on pieces of paper, put them in an empty teacup and drew so as to make up two mixed singles: Richard against Miss Snell and himself against Portia. F.J. said, "Are you a good player, Miss Menant?"

"I dare say you'll find out, Mr Dobbs."

He came to her place and stood behind her, put a hand on her shoulder and leaned down, with that sad, gentle smile of his, to speak in her ear. "Because I have no chivalry, Miss Menant. I gobble up nice young ladies like you."

Richard could not help laughing. No-one else, he observed, with a little surprise, had been – the word tickled came into his mind – tickled as he had been by the drollery in F.J.'s voice. Mr Menant and Mr Argent had suddenly begun to talk to each other and Mr Redington was frowning at his plate, as over some statistical problem he had just recalled.

They began their tournament at ten o'clock. Richard did not stand up for long against the smashing volleys of Miss Snell. He had, indeed, the impression that he was the target for a stream of small grey cannonballs fired at him with immense velocity, perhaps in the cause of women's rights. The rapid and humiliating end of the contest was a happy release for him. He and his opponent yielded the court to the other couple.

The second match was, alas, as uneven; more so, for as soon as Portia saw what she was up against she demonstratively ceased to try, and strolled sulkily about the court knocking balls back for her opponent to score more points with.

If the muscular Miss Snell had been impelled to treat every stroke of her racquet as a hammer blow against the oppressors of her sex, it was less easy to divine what force drove F.J., for he played as if a demon possessed him. His whole soul was in the game. He crouched, sprang, slammed with his racquet, sprinted to meet the ball, dived to make strokes. And although it was clear after the first seconds that he was playing against no opposition to speak of, he greeted every point he scored with an extraordinary display of elation, jumping like a child, and shouting his joy with shining face to the two spectators. And at the end of the unequal game he threw his racquet up into the air and shouted, "Oh, hooray," as he caught it.

They all drank lemonade. Then F.J. and Miss Snell went in to play – for the championship, as F.J. put it. Richard sat on a garden bench next to Portia. He had run out of words and courage and so he affected an intense interest in the game, turning his head left and right and keeping his face immobile in a stare of fascinated involvement.

It was a stiff game, prolonged by lengthy rallies. F.J. indulged in his acrobatics, dashing away the beads of sweat that purled down his face. Miss Snell, cool as ever, hardly seemed to move, but her racquet was magically wherever the ball was. It seemed that they were in for a long hard contest.

Stiff with consciousness of Portia's presence, shut up in himself for fear of her, he was surprised by her voice.

"Don't you think it's horrid, at their age?"

"At their age?" What had surprised him was the unexpectedly friendly tone of her voice; and the calm openness of her look at him.

"They're just pretending to be young."

"I hadn't thought of it like that."

"I think growing old is awful."

And then to his astonishment he heard himself managing a grotesque sort of compliment. "Oh, Portia. You will never grow old."

"I wish it was true."

He marvelled. Never once in all their acquaintance had her voice when speaking to him been so oddly gentle. She reflected. He had the courage to look at her eyes. And the watercolour blue of the irises held him spellbound. She said, "I didn't know you were capable of such eloquence."

"I am—" And in his new wonderment he contrived to add, "—with encouragement."

"Ah, well," she said. "We shall see."

They lapsed into silence. His silence was, now, utterly happy. What a beautiful countryside this Sussex was, one of those regions where one can see the sky so immense that it seems too great a canopy for little England. The pale blue thinned to white where the highest veils of cloud hung, and in the bluer depths of the sky piled snowfields, glaciers, Alps of cumulus, cloven and patched by shadows of blue and grey. Elsewhere, in blue expanses of a marvellous clarity, drifted smaller floes and woolly white balls.

At the foot of these high, high heavens ran the line of the Downs, here rising in slightest gradient, here notched, here straight or downward sloping, but always clean-drawn against the sky. And the flanks were clean, scooped and sculpted, showing white scars of chalk among the cool English green.

It was a cooler day, despite the radiant presidency of the sun. Winds roamed and sported, and tiny larks tumbled from on high. Everything added to Richard's passive bliss; the long low lines of downland against the sky, the sky's seeming infinity, the soft burn of sunshine and the playful buffets of breeze, the *thunk* of the tennis ball, the sound of voices near at hand yet remote from his awareness, and the feeling – he did not have to look at her – that Portia sat next to him, and that she sat relaxed, acceptant of him.

A thin white line wandered up the flank of Long Down, a path. Up it crawled two tiny objects. He had walked up that way himself. He watched the progress of the walkers; and stared, his eyes dilating.

What he saw knocked the breath out of his chest. He saw a picture between him and Long Down. It was sharply defined upon the air and its colours were as strong, its details as clear, as in the child's picture book he had once loved in which the pirate captain crouched on bent knees with cutlass raised, in bright blue coat,

61

with bright pink face, sharp black patch on one eye, bright red handkerchief on his head, everything in bright crudely printed shapes.

It was the same picture he had last seen on Wednesday night. It was Aunt Marian's drawing-room; but how changed! One wall was only a jagged remnant like a piece of broken tooth and, where the rest of the wall had been, there was the serene blue sky of today and the ridge of Long Down.

The floor ended, too, like that; in a glimpse of joists and broken plank-ends and hanging ends of carpet. And the room – it was there, all the things he knew, the marble mantelpiece, the dark, resplendent undergrowth of foliage and flowers on the tapestry paper, Aunt Marian's chesterfield couch— But the couch balanced on the edge of the broken floor above what seemed to be emptiness. The mirror above the mantelpiece was shattered. The tapestry hung in strips from the wall. All the ornaments were smashed and scattered, all the cabinets overturned, broken. Dun brickdust lay upon everything.

And in the far corner from his point of view, propped up against the wall as if flung there, was the upper half of his Aunt Marian. Her eyes were open and she looked straight at him in surprise. Around her spread a pond of blood.

It was not there any more. He was looking at Long Down again and the vast English sky. He began to choke and hurried away. He managed to contain his nausea until he was in the house. Then he found a lavatory and retched for some time.

It took a long time to beat F.J., but at last his resolve

crumbled and Miss Snell routed him. She shook hands with him and strode away. She announced her intention of going for a walk to the village before luncheon.

F.J. came to the bench, mopping his face with a handkerchief. His mouth was turned down glumly. He said, "That woman is a machine. She is set in motion at six a.m. and continues unabated until ten p.m. One cannot play tennis with a machine."

"I should think not," said Portia.

"There is no fun in it," he said.

"I can see that."

"Once the fun goes out of a game I lose the desire to win."

"Otherwise I am sure you would have won."

"You are making fun of me, Miss Menant."

"I wouldn't dream."

"I do hate losing," he said, and laughed his pleasant laugh. Portia laughed, too.

"Tell me about yourself," he said.

"What shall I tell you?"

"Do you do anything besides decorating this very beautiful house?"

"Oh, I don't live here. I live in London. I go to lectures."

"That is better than nothing."

"Women who live in the country do not do nothing. My mother writes."

"Do you?"

"No."

"Thank God for that. What else can a woman in the country do? Receive guests? Arrange flowers?"

"You like to be well received as a guest. You enjoy the sight of nicely-arranged flowers."

"Imbecilities."

"I know you think that women ought to be doing their share of the world's work."

"You read my books?"

"I am not illiterate."

"Neither are you inarticulate, Miss Menant."

"What are you writing just now, Mr Dobbs? If one is allowed to ask."

"One is not allowed."

"I am sorry."

"But I shall tell you. Would you like to take me for a walk through your beautiful gardens?"

They rose and walked on a flagged path alongside the house. F.J. began to tell her the story of his new novel. He walked close to her and lowered his head confidentially, and when they turned the corner of the house, to walk past its front, he took her by the elbow.

They went up three brick steps and under a brick arch into a walled garden. Around a small lawn were flower beds, a designed riot of colours. Blooms of contrasting hues massed in banks, and amid them in clumps rose other flowers on tall stems. F.J. breathed deeply. "Your gardeners mingle scents as well as colours."

"They do what my mother tells them."

"And look at the house in the sunlight. The charm of age. The tinge of moss on the red tiles. The stone mellowing from grey to yellow. The reward of privilege."

"It is the reward of my father's hard work."

"Your father's capital did the work."

"You talk like an old-fashioned disciple of Marx."

"Sometimes I am. And you know nothing at all about Marx except what you learned at my lectures."

"Perhaps you judge on insufficient acquaintance."

"One glance is enough to judge a young woman like you. Immensely pretty though you are."

"I suspect you do not like me, Mr Dobbs."

"Do you like me?"

"Should I?"

"I am a fubsy little man, am I not?"

"I have not said so."

"Oh, yes, I am small, my skin is pasty and my health is poor, though you would not think it when I play games. And do you know why I am all this? Because I was underfed and ill-fed from birth to the start of manhood, when it was too late to mend, and I was kept in damp gloomy basement rooms and damp dark attics and spent my youth behind shop counters under gaslight breathing foul air. If I had been brought up like your father or young Mr Latt, I would be a big, strong, pink brute like them."

"Such a great man and so sorry for himself."

"You are spoiled, Miss Portia."

"Am I?"

"But I like a girl with a bit of cheek."

"Do you, Mr Dobbs?"

Portia was not ignorant of the town's gossip and she was intrigued to know what turn the conversation would take; but at this moment Mr and Mrs Argent came into the walled garden, and Mr Argent, with a triumphant, "Ah," of discovery and a finger pointed biblically up at the sky, presumably in triumph at having found potential listeners, advanced upon them.

Richard went to his room and lay down. He had a great fear that he was mad. These pictures had begun after his misadventure last January.

65

As to that misadventure, he had not told anyone the truth of it. The robbery had not been fortuitous. He had been staying at the settlement in the Whitechapel Road. It was an evening of dense and sulphurous yellow fog. Nobody came for classes that evening and he lay upon his bed seized by one of his periodic fits of misery.

His body tormented him. He tried to live a busy life. Idleness let in the lusts of the flesh. He had taken to heart the admonitions of preachers and schoolmasters during his boyhood, not out of religious fervour but out of simple fear. It was so dangerous to fall. One heard of – indeed, one knew of – men who had gone with women and caught the loathly taint.

This fear had kept him virgin even throughout his years in Germany, a time of many allurements. Luckily he had enjoyed the friendship of another young Englishman, a fervent scholar and a devout Christian, whose company had providentially filled up his time and kept him clear of the temptations.

Yet the more he exercised, took cold baths, busied himself, the more healthy he felt himself to be, the more frenzied the fits that came upon him once in a while when he was alone. Sometimes he felt within a hair's breadth of falling, even if it were to take the briefest and most degrading relief with the most raddled, the most repellent of all those women who wore paint and big gaudy hats and gave him insolent invitations in the street.

It was all the harder on this January day because he had lately, on three occasions, seen a girl who was not like the others. She was small, slender, pale, pretty, plainly dressed. He could not believe she was what she appeared to be. She stood in the deep archway of a slum courtyard and when he passed she looked at him, not with a smile, but with a long, timid, imploring look that followed him. When he looked round he saw that she had turned her head to look after him.

He told himself (lying then on his bed as he was lying now) that she was beseeching him for help. She could be rescued. She could be taken away from this life. He was a coward not to stop, to talk to her, to try.

He knew that all this was a deliberate self-deceit. He knew what he wanted from her. His body raged. So, that evening, deceiving himself, in search of the quenching moment, driven desperate beyond the restraint of his fears, unable to stop himself, he walked like a mechanical man through the fog and found her.

He stopped and forced a few words out of his constricted throat. He asked her where she lived. She said it was not far, and without another word flitted away into the fog. He hurried to keep up with her. They walked for some minutes, how many he did not know, for time seemed everlasting. He felt damned, going to his doom. At last she turned from the Whitechapel Road into another arched entry. He went with her. There was a stunning shock on the right side of his head, behind the ear. He woke up in the London Hospital. His wallet was gone.

When he came up through the headache and understood what had happened, his first feeling was one of relief. He had not done that awful thing. He had been saved from the taint. He did not tell the police about the girl and he never tried to find her again. Aunt Marian came to commiserate and so, in due course, did all his friends.

*   *   *

Then there were the pictures. He could not call them dreams. Nothing happened in them. They were all as boldly defined and coloured as the one he had seen this morning.

There was, for instance, The Blacks. It was because he thought of them as pictures that he had given them titles, which he wrote in his mind starting with capital letters.

The Blacks was one of the most terrifying pictures. In it an army of soldiers faced him. They were not moving, but he could see that they were advancing at a trot, in wide ranks. They were black men, big, powerful bony men with terrible Congolese faces, skull faces with high cheekbones and concave cheeks, thick lips, broad noses and implacable eyes. The mystifying thing about this picture was that although they were blacks – clearly some kind of savage African blacks from that darkest centre of a dark continent – The Heart of Darkness – he had read the story – they wore yellow drill uniforms of a European type, with long trousers, bush jackets with flap pockets, and hats with floppy wide brims like Australian bushwhackers. And it was not assegais they carried, but rifles and machine-guns – some machine-guns were oddly-shaped thin-barrelled affairs which he recognised only by the cartridge belts hung round the soldiers' necks, others had fat, water-cooled snouts of a type he had seen in magazine photographs. They were still as he stared at the picture, but behind the wide front rank was another and another and another, jogging on at the double, packed close, stretching away to infinity, like a whole terrible continent overrunning – what?

But they only formed the left-hand mass of the

picture. The right-hand side was made up of jungle, a dark-green tangle of trees, creepers, patches of flaring coloured flowers, a dense struggle of vegetation for existence towering up against a sky baked by heat and flooded by sunlight to a sort of electrified blue, pale but steeped in colour, such as he had never seen in England.

The focus of the picture was in the middle. Between the jungle and the soldiers was a serpentine river. The column of soldiers wound along one bank to infinity. The jungle followed the other bank to infinity. And the river in between was wide, of a thick, clayey colour, running rapidly, and mingled with streams of dark red blood. Although the river was still in the picture one could tell that it ran rapidly by the swirl of currents, and it was dotted with black lumps. These black lumps were naked negro bodies, chopped up in every conceivable way, headless, limbless, riven open, torsos, haunches. They were numerous beyond counting. They dotted the river throughout its bends all the way back to infinity. So the soldiers advanced everlastingly in the picture and the river ran towards him everlastingly and it carried towards him these hacked carcases without number. And it ran with blood.

Another picture was less dramatic. For no reason that he could name, he found it as frightening as The Blacks. He called it The Man In The Mud.

It consisted of a landscape of mud. Here and there the splintered remnant of a tree-trunk leaned against a sky leaden with rain. The mud was dotted with round pools of water that gleamed silver. There must have been hundreds of them. Between the pools were clumps of barbed wire, fearful tangles of it. No farmer would have left any of his wire in such a mess. In the fore-ground of the picture was a large pool of water; made larger, of course, by its place in the perspective. On its farther rim a veritable thicket of barbed wire was supported on many small irons. Draped upon the wire was the body of a man, with its back to Richard. The body was dressed in what must have been a khaki uniform, which hung now misshapenly upon the dead man. Perhaps the dead soldier was British, for although his feet were in the water of the pool he wore puttees of the British type and the rifle which lay half-sunk in the mud beside him was a British Lee-Enfield, such as Richard had often seen carried stiffly at the slope by those six-foot Guardsmen who stamped up and down outside Buckingham Palace. No wound was visible but a great rusty stain of blood had spread upon the surface of the pool.

There were many other pictures. If they had done no more than appear they would have been perplexing and unnerving enough; how much more so now that two of them had turned out to be prophecies!

The first picture to come true was The Fallen Horse. In this, a cart-horse had fallen down. It had been freed from the traces and lay in the roadway at the corner of a street that led into a wider street. The picture was as bright and crowded with detail as a painting by Frith. There was the crowd of passers-by, the shops, even with their names clear upon their fascias, the traffic held up, taxis, hansoms, buses with passengers on their open top decks all standing up to crane their necks, each figure perfectly limned – indeed, photographed; and, held up by the crowd in the foreground, a pony and trap in which sat a Pearly King and Queen, Cockneys in the finery that certain of them wore on public holidays, black velvet costumes covered with mother-of-pearl buttons.

The onlookers at the front of the crowd formed an irregular ring, pressing back to leave a space. It was not the two policemen present who held them back, but fear of the blood on the roadway. The horse had been knocked down in a collision. Its chest had been split open. Blood lay upon the road like a thick outpouring of gloss paint.

On Easter Monday, at the corner of Percy Street and Tottenham Court Road, Richard had come upon this sight. Everything was as in the picture. The location was unmistakably the same. The names on the shop fronts were the same. Everything and everyone stood in the same position. He recognised faces. Next to him, as he stood there with his heart thumping away, was the pony and trap. The Pearly King was shouting to a policeman to clear a way for him. The Pearly Queen was declaiming woefully to the crowd that they only wanted to get to 'Ampstead 'Eath.

Unmistakable. No question of coincidence. Richard had already consulted doctors but there was no question of a doctor here; unless, perhaps, he was suffering one kind of hallucination upon another and he had need of an alienist.

Given time, terror dissipates. Mental turbulence subsides. In time one can always pacify one's self with some sort of explanation. Richard eventually persuaded himself that he had witnessed some kind of extreme, extraordinary coincidence. Moreover, since the picture of The Fallen Horse had not since recurred, he was able to remind himself that memory plays tricks. The picture,

71

he assured himself, had *not* been the exact replica of
the scene. He had only re-remembered it, so to speak,
after he had seen the real accident, so that his memory
of the picture was a falsified one. No, no, it must have
been different. If only he could reach beyond the tricks
of memory, he would discover that it had not been at
all the same as the real event.

He had done nothing about the pictures for some time.
Some after-effect of the sandbagging, he assumed. But
when they had continued throughout February he had
gone – no question of telling Aunt Marian and he had
no friend close enough for confidences – to the family
doctor, who in turn, after hearing his account, had
sent him to a brain surgeon, who had assured him that
there was no evidence of damage or symptom of concussion. His behaviour, his reactions to tests, were all
perfectly normal.

The pictures had gone on. And at the end of March,
after more frights than he could stand, he had gone
again to Doctor Hall, who had this time asked him
questions about his life. Did he go with women? Had
he really not broken his duck? "No? Just as well. I don't
want you coming to me with a chancre. You keep away
from the bad ones, my boy. But get married. Find a nice
girl and marry. That's your trouble. Too much on the
brain. Bad dreams."

"It isn't dreams, doctor," he protested.

"Of course it's dreams. We all know the kind of
dream in which you think you're awake. Off you go,
my boy. Marry a good girl. Ask me to the wedding."

He had not gone back to the doctor; nor told anyone
else. He was frightened that someone might want to

send him to an alienist. All this, of course, had been before the picture of The Fallen Horse came true.

Now imagine the effect on poor Richard of the incident of the knocked-down child, on the day he came to Ashtons. For that, too, he had seen in a picture, only six nights before.

That was why, to the puzzlement of Borrett the chauffeur, he had prowled up and down the lane, examining the scene. It was all the same. The child was the same child. The patch of blood in the dust was the same size and shape. There was also the red notice-board on the tree.

Somehow, he had got over that, too. Doctor Hall had counselled (in the interim, presumably, before he found a good girl to marry) plenty of rest and distraction, and Richard had determined to seek rest and distraction at Ashtons. He had calmed himself with inward cries of, "Nonsense!" "Deluding yourself." "You never saw any such picture." There were times when he told himself that he might still be suffering from some mild concussion effect. The brain surgeon had told him that one could never entirely be sure; only time would tell. It would all wear off. The great thing was to carry on normally.

Richard now considered once more whether he might be going mad; or at least in some way mentally astray. Once again he convinced himself that this could not be so. His thoughts were entirely reasonable. His behaviour was unfailingly normal. He was his old self. Demonstrably, incontrovertibly, there was nothing at all wrong with him; except that the pictures appeared before him.

And what was he to make of the – as he insisted he must call them – coincidences?

He had missed luncheon. A maid knocked at his door. She brought a note from Mrs Menant. A party had been got up (by F.J.? he wondered) to visit a notable garden in the district. Would he care to come? He scribbled a polite refusal on the note. The maid went off. Later he heard the sound of voices and of motor-cars. The motor-cars drove away. He looked out of the window. Portia was reading by the lily pond.

Solitude, he decided, was damnation. He washed and made himself presentable. He went downstairs to join Portia, remembering, fearfully, F.J.'s advice about audacity.

Six

Portia was reading an article in an art magazine. It told her that pictures were not about anything. They were only examples of something called Abstract Harmony. Portia, a passionless girl in most respects, had one passion, if an imperious longing can be called a passion – to be up-to-date, to do all the up-to-date things, to hold all the newest opinions. Her friends all talked about Abstract Harmony and she was determined to be as glib on the subject as any of them.

The sun was too bright, the touch of the breeze was too playful for her to read with any application. She saw Richard and was glad to put down her magazine.

She was herself in a playful mood, unusually light of heart. Her walk with F.J. had aroused in her a vague sense of flirtation. It was a most agreeable feeling, tickling one's interior, as it were, making one want to smile. She enjoyed it sufficiently to want to prolong it, and at the sight of Richard it occurred to her that he might do for the purpose.

The thought came to her without malice. She had nothing against Richard except that he was young, and she considered young men to be foolish. All the young men of her acquaintance, in their various ways, were, although some of them were officially considered to be clever young men. Richard was not of the lowest, silly ass, stratum. Once in a while he blurted out an intelligent remark. The trouble was the blurting out. That was all he did, with her; or he talked doggedly and dully about, oh, topics. His fair hair brushed down smoothly to its cropped edges tended to come unstuck and protrude like handfuls of straw. Excitement or heat made his pink fair skin turn scarlet. His shoulders were broad and he looked powerful, but he ought to have been a little taller. He was not greatly promising, but since he was silly about her he might provide a little more practice.

Richard sat down next to her on the bench and marvelled at the brightness of her smile. He said, "Hallo again."

"What on earth happened to you this morning?"

"Bit unwell."

"I should think so. You bolted."

" 'Fraid so. Awfully sorry."

"And left me alone with that horrid fat little man."

"F.J.?"

"There are other horrid men here. He is the only one who runs to fat."

"I wish you would see his good points."

"I can. As a writer. Besides, he's too old to go cavorting about."

"He's only forty-one."

She turned that new smile on him again. "I prefer the company of twenty-one."

"Oh. Actually, I'm twenty-two."

"Excellent. Maturity without senility."

They laughed.

"I thought you must have been unwell when you didn't come down to lunch," she said. "Are you better?"

"Yes, thanks." A second went by. He groped for talk

76

and found the magazine on the bench. "I say, I've read this. It's jolly interesting."

"Don't say 'jolly'. You know who it reminds me of."

"Sorry."

"And don't keep saying 'sorry'. You're always saying 'sorry'."

"It is interesting, though."

"I thought the Post-Impressionist Exhibition was marvellous."

"So did I. I wish we could have gone together. I'd already seen a lot of modern paintings in Germany. In Munich. I'm all for them."

"So am I."

"I think they're fearfully exciting."

"So do I."

"Well, you see, you have to look for the emotional significance—"

"Which is the most important subject matter of art. An abstract harmony of line and colour. Rhythm."

"Yes. You know, all this literary stuff is useless. The Departing Emigrant and all that rot."

"It is all rot. It's simply not art. A good rocking-horse has more of the true horse about it than a . . ."

"—An instantaneous photograph of a Derby winner." He interrupted in his eagerness to show that he, too, had Mr Fry by heart.

"Exactly. And the way they go on! The dreadful things they say! I mean, the newspapers."

"Sheer ignorance," Richard said, "but only to be expected. It's worse in Germany. The artists get mobbed there, and beaten in the streets, and called traitors."

"The majority will always be ignorant. It is only the few who can appreciate. Look at Diaghilev."

77

"Oh, that was marvellous, too. So many marvellous things."

"And Shaw and Chekhov and all that. It's only the few with the sensitive—"

He supplied the word. "—Aura."

"Yes, that's it."

Oh, this was the time for audacity! For were not he and she now agreed that they were of the sensitive minority, the few who possessed that aura? "I say," he said. "I hope I'm not being too earnest."

"Earnest?"

"You said this morning that I was always earnest."

"A compliment, surely."

"You meant I was rather a bore."

"Well—" She trailed off and then turned a radiant little smile up at him, making it a joke between them.

"I expect I am usually. But I haven't meant to be."

"Haven't you?"

"No. You see, whenever we've met – you know, Hyde Park and all that – well, I think it was shyness really."

"Do I make you shy?"

"Yes."

"Now?"

"No. That's the wonderful thing."

"Isn't that nice?" she said. "Let's go for a walk."

Transported, he stood up with her and, even more transported, he felt her slip a hand under his arm. Her hand guided him past the lily pond, to a path which ran between tall yew hedges to a gate in the garden wall.

"You see," he said, "I never could think of anything to talk about, except some book or other, or the Science Museum."

"Oh, the Science Museum." She made it sound like an immensely witty remark and they both laughed.

"I just used to talk on. About anything. I think I bored myself stiff. Let alone you."

"At least we suffered together," she said, and they laughed again.

"Now be un-earnest," she said.

"Un-earnest?"

"Be amusing."

"Oh, Lord."

"What's the matter?"

"How does one be amusing?"

"Try."

"Heavens, shall I crack jokes like a music-hall comic?"

"No. But you're improving."

"Or do a merry little jig?"

"I'd like to see that—"

"Ah—"

"But not now."

They went through the gate and across a bridge over a stream with deep banks, into a wood. "This is all part of the garden really," Portia said. "That's father's trout stream and, wild though this wood may look, he's stocked it with all sorts of rare trees. Look at this one."

They stopped.

"It's called a balsam poplar. Pluck a leaf. Now squash it. Like this, between your fingers. Now smell it."

"Lovely," he said. "It smells of honey."

"It's best here in the Spring. The whole wood is covered in flowers. It's like a carpet. Daffs, anemones, everything you can imagine."

Enchantment. A child's swing hung by ropes from the branch of an oak. "Was this yours?"

"No. I was too big for swings when we came here. The last people left it."

"Where did you live when you were a child?"

"In Streatham. In an absolutely awful huge enormous dreadful house three times as big as this one and all red brick. It had ghastly huge laurel shrubberies all round it and it was called The Laurels."

"I lived in India when I was a very little boy."

"Did you like it?"

"Oh, Lord, yes, my mother and father were alive. I can remember them ever so well—" He stopped.

"Poor old Richard."

She was wonderful.

He was able to speak once more. "We had a bungalow up at Simla. My father fixed a swing up in the doorway. This one made me think of it. It seemed ever so much nicer than a swing in a tree. I don't know why."

She sat in the swing, her back to him. "Swing me. Go on – give me a push."

He advanced his hands but he could not touch her body. He took the ropes, pulled the swing back and launched her. As she swung back she cried, "Give me a push – not the rope, it joggles."

"Sorry." He had checked her. This time he put his hands flat against the small of her back and pushed, and she swung, and he pushed again and she swung again.

She called, "Higher—" and he pushed hard, now, again and again, feeling her slender body in his hands for a moment each time before she went away from him.

"That's enough."

He stood back and watched her come to rest. She sat in the swing with her back to him. They were silent for a few seconds but this time he did not mind it. Without turning round she asked him if he had read a novel that F.J. had published a couple of years ago. It was about a university teacher, a married man, who lived with a girl student of his. It had caused a great sensation; from some quarters, cries of outrage as violent as those evoked by the Post-Impressionist paintings. Of course, to a large number of younger people it had become a banner.

"Oh, yes," Richard said.

"What do you think of it?"

"I approve. I approve absolutely of what that couple did. He was married unhappily. He couldn't get a divorce. Why not? It was an ethical marriage really, wasn't it?"

She said, "I have a friend who has done that."

"Have you really?"

"She has joined her life to that of a married man. I go to tea with them."

"I say, do you?"

"I make no secret of it and I have let my parents know. I brook no interference with my freedom."

"I should say not."

"I believe in freedom."

"So do I."

"For intelligent adults, mind you."

"Oh, absolutely."

"I'll tell you what," she said. "Would you mind very much kissing me?"

Panic clutched at his heart. He felt the drench of heat up through his face. She said, "You look rather funny now."

He said, "Keep still."

She kept still, hands at her side, lips pursed. He put his head forward, keeping his hands at his side, and touched her lips with his. Her lips were cool.

She said, "No. Absolutely nothing. All that rot in books. I don't think you've had much experience, have you?"

He said, "None. I'm awfully sorry."

She said, "Don't men—?"

"None. Really."

She said, "I thought men were supposed to go with certain women and pay them for it, and I think that's rather horrible. I'm rather glad if you haven't."

"Oh," he said. "I'm afraid you thought me an awful fool."

"Not at all. May I try?"

"Yes, of course."

He stood, almost, to attention, but lowered his head. She put her lips on his. She lingered close to him and her lips spread over him. They were warm and soft now.

They came apart. He put his hands lightly on her waist and kissed her mouth lightly. The kiss mattered less than feeling her waist between his hands. He pulled her close and kissed her again, and this time it was hard and rough and he moved his mouth clumsily, seeking.

She pushed hard. "No." It was harsh and breathless. "No, no, no—"

He stood away from her. "Oh— I am sorry."

"I expect I led you on." She was curt.

"Not at all. It was my fault."

"It was mine absolutely," she said. "Please don't patronise. Please treat me as an intelligent, modern person."

"Oh, I will," he promised. "I will, really."

"Good," she said. "Then we will say no more about it. You saw Pavlova with your aunt, I believe."

"Oh, yes. Aunt Marian loved her."

"And what do you think of her?"

They walked back to the lawn, not arm-in-arm, and there Portia commanded tea. They sat and talked about topics until the motor-car party arrived home. It was an earnest conversation but Richard did not care. He was happy.

Seven

"Mr Latt—"

Mrs Redington stood in the doorway of the drawing-room, in which Richard sat reading *Tristram Shandy*. "What an extraordinary coincidence," she said, and came to sit down next to him. "I was just now thinking of you."

He put his book down on a small table. "Of me?"

Footfalls reverberated on upstairs floors. Water could be heard running and splashing; and occasionally a snatch of muffled voices. The excursionists had retired to their quarters; there, Richard had hoped, to remain until dinner-time. But here was one of them, with a glow upon her that suggested both that she had bathed and that she was eager for conversation.

"I have been told," she said, "that, although you perform most helpful work for a socialist organisation, you have not yet embraced the socialist faith."

"Faith," Richard said. "Well, there is the Christian faith."

Mrs Redington was thin. She had a fringe of curls. She inhabited a long garment made by a country crafts-woman. "I impugn no religious faith, but do you not think that there can also be a social faith?"

A Siamese cat came to Richard's rescue. It pushed open the unfastened door, glided across the room like a streak of smoke and jumped on to the settee next to

Richard. It curled up there and fastened a glittering gaze upon Richard to tell him that he was intruding upon a private preserve. "Sorry, old thing," Richard said, tried to stroke the cat and withdrew his hand from teeth showing in a silent snarl. "Beautiful things," he said to Mrs Redington, "but you can never make friends with them."

"A social faith, Mr Latt."

"Faith. That's a bit of a poser."

" 'Bring me my bow of burning gold.' "

"Oh, yes," Richard said. "I know. They don't talk much about faith at the Fabian. It's all statistics. Terribly impressive when you hear them but I'm afraid I always forget them by the time I get home."

"Since I am a Fabian myself, and also a statistician, I know well what you mean. But will you not tell me what it is that stands between you and socialism?"

Richard laughed. "You know, Mrs Redington, I have been asked that question two or three times by evangelists. Only they ask what stands between me and perfect faith?"

"You are quite a nice young man when you open your mouth. But I will not let you beg my question."

"Oh, laziness, I suppose."

"How sad! Laziness is the one vice that neither my husband nor I can abide."

"Why?"

"Because it is a waste of the most precious thing we have. Life. The time we have to live. I talk of physical sloth, it is also true of mental laziness like yours, which puts off decisions which might lead to fruitful activities."

"But why is it a vice, Mrs Redington? Is it not a

simple freedom, to live as we wish? If it's not to the harm of others."

"If you hold back from the betterment of mankind you are doing harm to others."

"I'm afraid I'm not at all sure about sins of omission. There are some undeniable ones. But how many are just a matter of opinion? And what a weapon they are in the hands of busybodies."

"You think me a busybody."

"Oh, no, Mrs Redington. Oh, my goodness, no—"

"But I am. A notorious busybody. I am a thorn in the flesh of all sorts of people. I rather think I shall be a thorn in your flesh until you make up your mind. The more I see of you the more you impress me."

Flattery from a woman was new to Richard. It made him hot and confused. "I – I'm most grateful—"

"What for?"

"For your interest."

"But you would rather go on as you are because you are quite comfortable, thanks very much."

"Honestly, yes."

"Yes."

"Also, there are so many kinds of socialism, it seems to me."

"Socialism only means one thing. The putting of the social interest first. Do you agree with that?"

"Yes, but—"

"Of course there are all sorts of ridiculous sects that put all sorts of ridiculous interpretations upon that definition. There is Mr Keir Hardie, who has a considerable following of young clerks and earnest workmen, particularly in the northern counties, who believes that waving a red flag will bring the millennium—"

"I was going to say that Mr Asquith and Mr Lloyd George would both claim that they were putting the social interest first."

"You know better than that, my lad. You know very well that the old parties represent sections, the Tories the landed interest, the Liberals in general the business interest. All the politicians find it expedient to introduce reforms, both to allay discontent and to buy votes. And I suppose out of some lurking sense of charity. Mr Lloyd George goes further than the others, because he is more unscrupulous in seeking votes. But think of the dreadful want that remains in this country. Good heavens, Mr Latt, would you like me to take you to see some of it?"

"I do live a good deal in the East End of London."

"Indeed you do. I had forgotten. All the more reason why you should make up your mind."

"I suppose so."

"My husband and I place a great deal of importance on the recruitment of young men like you."

"Like me?"

"Young men of intelligence and good family. They will be the framework of socialism. Those who tell us that socialism will be achieved overnight, by some fearful upheaval—"

"Jack London."

"You read upon the subject, I see— They do us no service. It is a matter of gradually, gradually, gradually, by the establishment of municipal services, by the extension of governmental interest in matters that are at present the concern of private charity—"

"Remorseless melioration."

"Thanks to my husband, that has become something of a watchword."

"Yes, indeed."

"As people become used to the elementary public services – the provision of water, the removal of sewage, without any payment except through taxation – so they will become used to socialism. It will come upon the nation before the nation has realised what it is. And it will all be the work of the Civil Service."

"I see."

"The Civil Service in which my husband, of course, already plays a considerable part. Dismiss from your mind any nonsense about the Worker Resurgent. We all know the British working-man. There will be room for a certain number of working-men who have sufficiently educated themselves. More and more, I hope, as education is improved. And we shall have to civilise a sufficient number of labour leaders so that they may take their place among cultivated people and indeed, one day, at Court. But in the main the standard-bearers of socialism will be gentlefolk."

"Gentlefolk," Richard said.

"And now, what are we going to do about you?"

Richard put a hand out to the cat. Even a scratch would have helped. But the cat deserted him. It jumped down, wreathed across the room and disappeared sinuously through the narrow opening of the door.

"I do not believe that you are lazy," Mrs Redington said. She leaned towards him and placed the tip of her forefinger on his knee, just above the cap. "It is simply" – tap – "a question" –tap – "of inertia."

"Inertia."

"Inertia arising from your fear of making such a

88

crucial decision. My dear Mr Latt, I understand you—"
Leaning towards him, her face close to his, she smiled,
her eyes looking into his. "I understand young men so
well."

"Do you?"

She had four fingertips resting on his leg above the
knee now, and they absent-mindedly played a little
tune. "I do, I do indeed. You will come to tea with me,
Mr Latt – when we are back in London."

"Oh, that *is* kind of you."

"I shall adopt you."

"Oh, thank you."

"You will come to see the light."

"I shall listen most attentively to everything you say."

"And you will be company for me."

"Oh," Richard said deprecatingly. "Me!"

"Why do you refer to yourself in that tone?"

"All the brilliant people you must meet—"

"My dear boy – my very dear, charming young
man—" Her hand, now lying upon his leg, emphasised
the compliment with the most brief and gentle of
squeezes. "Brilliant people are a bore sometimes. My
husband, excellent man, is shut in his office with Blue
Books until the small hours too often. Far too often. There
are times when I am a lonely person."

"Oh, no, Mrs Redington."

"Oh, yes, Mr Latt." And this time she smiled with
such warmth, and accompanied the smile with a squeeze
that although brief was of such heartiness that even
Richard became aware that something other than
sociology was in question. There was an instant eruption
inside him of astonishment compounded with gratifica-
tion. Governed now only by panic, he stood up abruptly.

"It's been awfully interesting and I shall come to see you – if you will be so kind as to ask me. I—" He groped in his waistcoat pocket for his watch. "Oh, dear, the time – you see, I am supposed to meet – I am supposed to meet Mr Dobbs – for billiards before dinner. I wonder if—"

She regarded him with a smile of lazy, entire comprehension. "Of course I excuse you. Mr Dobbs is not a man whom one keeps waiting. Run along, Mr Latt."

Richard went into the billiard room and was smitten by the same shock he used to experience as a child whenever his Nanny pointed to some happening that appeared to prove the truth of the adage that Liars Never Prosper; for F.J. was in the room alone, knocking a ball about on the table. He at once proposed a hundred up and Richard, feeling himself the victim of fatality, took a cue.

Richard, normally not bad at billiards, played ineptly, his mind disorganised. F.J. took his time over every shot, prowling about the table, sighting, trying the cue-rest, chuckling in quiet triumph as he propelled the balls in marvellous geometrical rebounds to make long breaks.

"I've been talking with Mrs Redington in the drawing-room," Richard said.

"Sh!" Crouched, concentrated, F.J. made a shot. He straightened up, expelled a long sigh of satisfaction and chalked his cue. "That old rattlesnake."

"Rattlesnake?"

"I see you're not much acquainted with the vernacular. Did she put her hand inside your flies?"

Richard said, "Oh—" and waited while F.J. made another shot.

"I had her when I was twenty-five," F.J. said. "Week my first book was published and got good reviews. She's hot on success. Hot generally. Had to shake her off, though. Are you going in for her?"

"I? Oh, you see, I haven't thought—"

"You could do worse for experience. But don't get in the coils. Not in the coils—. No, young Richard, on second thoughts, you're too much of an innocent. Look elsewhere."

"Yes. Yes. Thank you."

F.J. chuckled again, as if at a memory. "But perhaps you're not such an innocent after three years in Germany. Eh?"

"No. No."

"I should think not. Those sweet Rhine Maidens. All those accommodating serving wenches at the inns. I wonder if they employ them with that in mind."

"Oh, yes. I wonder."

"Used to go on walking tours. When the money was short. Fine times. Swiss Alps. Vosges. Black Forest. Ah, splendid, that, splendid. Healthy. Simple food, walk your feet sore, sunrise and sunset, peaks and pine forests. I sigh for those days. And in the evening, after dinner— one was never let down. Never. Always a warm little armful in one's bed. If one wasn't too tired."

"Yes. Yes. I know. It's extraordinary."

"Mind you, one had to be careful. I hope you were."

"Careful?"

"You haven't come back with anything you regret?"

"No. No."

"Not a matter for neglect anywhere. One man in

seven, the doctors tell me. But specially so in Germany, for some reason. Nietzsche. Heine. You know."

"Oh, yes."

"Take my advice, young Richard. Wash. Wash promptly. Never let the circumstances embarrass you. A strong solution of permanganate."

"I see." It should be said that this was Richard's first house party; in fact, his first exposure to the company of people older than himself other than tea-party guests in Aunt Marian's drawing-room, who did not speak like this. Of course he had heard the talk of fellow-schoolboys and fellow-students. Somehow he had acquired the illusion that serious grown-ups, and especially important grown-ups, did not talk like this.

"Of course," F.J. said, "I am not talking about the respectable ladies with whom one dallies. One has no worries there."

"No. Of course not."

F.J. moved the pointer on the score-board past the winning mark. "Another game? – Ah—"

From the hall downstairs came the concussions and deep echoes of the dressing gong. Richard went to his room, lost in wonderment at the novel events and conversations of this day.

The novelties of the day were not ended. There are times when, after an uneventful life, one is astonished by the number of things that can happen in a single day. This, it seemed to Richard, was such a day.

Portia made another late entrance to the drawing-room before dinner, after Hawker had been sent to give a tactful touch to the dressing-gong especially for her.

She wore a different evening dress, in the same style as last night's but this time of pale blue, with a tasselled girdle under the waist and softening mist of gauze overlay. Miss Snell said, "Poiret suits you, my dear."

Portia smiled at her and then, wonderfully, at Richard, in the most natural, ordinary way, as a girl does to someone who is in her confidence. He was enchanted.

In the planning of her dinner Mrs Menant did not try to compete with the great hostesses. She did not have a chef or a pâtissier; only, as she often told her guests, a good plain English woman who cooked good English food, much of which came from the house farm, the fish new-caught in local waters.

Tonight the good plain English woman had excelled herself, and Mr Menant had provided memorable wines. Richard ate and drank with gusto, excited by Portia's smile. The food and wine heightened his excitement.

The theme of the talk – table talk at Mrs Menant's was always on some serious theme – was progress. This led inevitably to the moment when Mr Argent felt that the time was ripe for his oration, the oration which he had delivered to so many Mechanics' Institutes and trade union meetings. "Civilisation," Mr Argent fluted, "is now on the march and that march will never be halted. Every step endows it with more strength for a further advance. We have entered the era of peace, for even the most stupid now perceive that war is too destructive to be entertained even as a possibility. We have entered the era of plenty – yes, my dear friends—"

He paused and looked questioningly at his hostess.

"More lemonade for Mr Argent," she commanded. Mr Argent drank nothing but lemonade. He had another oration about drink, which he believed to be invented by the devil to turn men into beasts, and the curse of the working class; a belief for which he merited some sympathy, for as a child he had been beaten almost senseless every Saturday night and seen his mother reduced to a wreck by his drunken father, a Norwich ropemaker. He was also the only person at the table, with the exception of his wife, who did not do justice to the fare. He required small portions and ate them daintily, with many painstaking and ceremonious manipulations of knife and fork. It created the impression that he was a man whose concerns were chiefly spiritual. His wife asked for even smaller helpings – she was the kind of dear who asked the maids for teeny-weeny bits – and ate as finickingly as her husband, all the time casting glances at him as if her role in life was to imitate him in all things, and to listen, for she hardly spoke.

"Thank you," said Mr Argent, and took an orator's sip, " – we have entered the era of plenty despite the ubiquitous evidences of dreadful poverty of which we are all too aware, nay, which all of us – almost all of us, I should say – have made it our mission to publicise in the first place, to diminish at the fastest rate possible and in the course of God's good time, for I believe the endeavours of this age to be under the direction of the Almighty, to be abolished."

"Beautiful sentiments beautifully expressed," said Mrs Menant, and was about to fly another kite, but Mr Argent, skilled in such matters, was beforehand. He raised a hand and cried, "Abolished! Yes. Because modern science and modern machines have given us the means of providing an abundance of all mankind's needs. It is our cornucopia, if only we will use it. Ah—" A maid was at his elbow serving— "a wee, wee portion of asparagus only, if you please – thank you, my dear."

Mrs Redington whispered to Richard, "The work-people don't understand a thing he says but they do admire a man who uses long words like cornucopia. He has reached his present position on sheer verbosity."

"Yes," Mr Argent resumed, having tasted a tiny piece of asparagus, "we are certain of our future because we have a world order at last, a world order that is assured. In the vanguard of the march to progress is Europe, which has produced the highest of all human civilisations in the existence of man. In the vanguard of Europe is England. And let me say, to those who contest the patriotism of Labour, that I regard the supremacy of England as the prime condition of human progress."

Richard had sampled in varying quantities prawns, clear soup, fried smelts, lobster soufflé, sweetbreads, chicken à la Marengo, saddle of mutton and a sorbet, refusing many other offered dishes to make his choices. He now tackled his duck, and took some asparagus from the maid; with a good deal more to come. He had also drunk more sherry and champagne than he was used to, perhaps because of the proximity of Mrs Redington, who, if F.J.'s almost incredible suggestion was to be entertained, had actually made overtures to him. (But had she? Could she have? Did such people really do such things?)

Perhaps, too, he was a little intoxicated by Portia, who throughout Mr Argent's discourse had been ex-changing with him merry little grins of complicity. She was looking at him now, and this time the points of light in her eyes were positively a challenge, an instigation, in response to which he said, "Mr Argent, you talk of the supremacy of England, but what about America?"

"America? Do you mean the United States?" Mr Argent spoke in the faint, frail voice which some schoolmasters employ before they crush a venturesome pupil.

"Yes, sir."

"America – If the coarseness at table will be forgiven, the land of spittoons."

General laughter. F.J., who was profoundly occupied with a plate on to which he had commanded an immense quantity of duck to be heaped, grunted, "America is irrelevant."

"I absolutely agree," Mr Menant said. "They have great industries but an inexhaustible home market."

"They will go on with their graft and their lynchings," F.J. said. "They know or care nothing about the rest of the world. Why should they?"

Richard asked, "What about President Taft and his Arbitration Treaties?"

"They don't want trouble, that's all. It only proves my point."

"They lionise you on your lecture tours," Mrs Redington said.

"Ah," F.J. said, "read Dickens about that. Culture is one of the things vulgarians think they can buy. Hence the large fees which induce people like myself – and that poor wretch Oscar – to go."

Richard was now borne high on wine and on Portia's glances. Exultation flooded through his veins, and the desire to fly higher. "F.J.," he said, "don't you think all this talk about machines and progress is what's irrelevant?"

"How so?"

(Oh, he felt inside him, here goes!) "Because art is the only thing that matters."

He, the unregarded, the naked chick fallen out of the nest, had made an impact! For there was a flutter of cries and remarks of disagreement. He mattered! Portia's eyes were on him, wide and steady with expectation and support.

"Oh, that," said F.J., who never minded speaking with food in his mouth. "I've been polemising against that for twenty years."

"Then you've been polemising in vain," said Richard, prompted by Portia's eyes.

"Indeed?"

"Yes," Richard cried, full of glory that he was holding everybody's attention, "I want people not to be hungry and to have more food in them, but this will not bring redemption."

"Hear, hear," said Portia, elevating him to a higher plane of glory.

"Religion, Mr Latt," said Mr Argent.

"Filling their bellies will be a good start," said F.J.

"I suppose," Richard said, "most people will never be redeemed. But there are a few who have the possibility in them—" He looked at Mrs Redington—"and I don't just mean gentlefolk. There are a few people who may sometimes transcend all the bad things in life, who may even feel that it is worth enduring life, because sometimes they have a glimpse of beauty – it may be in music – or in the truth of a story – or in a painting. Or a very ordinary man in his garden."

97

"Beauty," F.J. grunted, and lowered his head to his food in dismissal of the subject.

"Well, well," said Mr Argent. "We have an orator in our midst."

This quenched Richard. He let the conversation flow on without him. But he was content. He and Portia had looked at each other across the table and her "Hear, hear" had given him the feeling that the two of them were joined together against the world.

"Goldstein paid fifty thousand pounds for his Hungarian baroness," Mr Menant said. "He got the two daughters thrown in for the price."

The men were alone after dinner. For some reason the talk after dinner last night had not run on these lines. Perhaps tonight they had all been more stimulated by food and drink. Richard sat wondering more and more as the talk went on. He had let Mr Menant give him a glass of brandy. He really should not have had it, but the wine had made him too sluggish to say "no." This talk was not like the student or schoolboy talk. There was no laughter or dirty-joking. It was an exchange of gossip in dry tones. Only Mr Argent took no part in it. He sat upright in a tall winged chair, his eyes lightly closed, the fingertips of one hand pressed on those of the other.

"Of course, he's impotent," Redington said. "A fellow at the club tells me that the three women advertise it to the world, and run a regular brothel into the bargain."

"But don't you know," F.J. squeaked, "that's what he wants? He watches. He has the place fixed up."

"And that's the man who would have bought himself

into the English peerage," Mr Menant said, "if Edward hadn't died."

Mr Argent, still in his attitude of prayer, gave voice. "Our new King will never stand for that."

Redington said, "There's always Lloyd George to put a word in."

"Dear me," F.J. said, "if you are going to take such a high moral tone you must fortify me with some more of your Armagnac— Enough, thank you. You appear to suggest, Menant, that Mr Goldstein's quirks disqualify him for preferment."

"I do not like the Goldsteins of this world."

"On what grounds?"

"Not on religious grounds, F.J. I do business with them. Some of them are decent enough fellows. I do not like the grubby little ones."

"Ah," F.J. said. He named an English duke who frequently went abroad to satisfy his taste for little girls, since this traffic had now become dangerous in Great Britain. He ran through a list of, so he alleged, homosexuals of eminence and ancient English descent (Richard all the while more and more stupefied with surprise, sipping his brandy to sustain himself and becoming all the more stupefied by it). He went into details of strange sexual practices of which Richard had never before heard, some of them, to him, sickening, and associated with them a bewildering assortment of churchmen, solid businessmen from Birmingham and Manchester with household names and no-nonsense reputations, university dignitaries and other well-known men.

And again Richard sat silent within a flow of conversation, a part of his world crumbling to pieces. The talk fuddled yet excited him, and he was excited, too, by the rank, dark smell of cigar smoke, which was like another smell beyond his experience but of which he was by instinct aware, and which worked upon him.

He remained in this state for the rest of the evening. When they joined the ladies in the drawing-room he found safety in a low armchair in the opposite corner to Portia's. He wanted to be as unobtrusive as a curled-up cat. He confined his talk to brief and modest replies.

Instead of seeking Portia's glances he avoided them. He had come to a state of high excitement and the reason he feared to see Portia was that inside his mind he was conducting excited, passionate conversations with her; or, rather, he was pouring out to her with all the new eloquence that he had discovered in himself at the dinner table this evening the story of his love for her, and she, in his mind, was making demure but lovingly affirmative responses. This imaginary dialogue had caused his whole interior being to resound with a great hymn of joy. He wanted to make it his reality. He could not bear to shatter it by looking across the room and meeting the glance, perhaps once more sulky or indifferent or simply bored, of the living Portia.

She seemed, indeed, to have become her old self once more, for she also remained quiet and her answers, when one or another guest tried to draw her into conversation, were so curt as to be rude. Rude, too, she was, when she rose suddenly, made her excuses and went out of the room.

Richard at once rose, the movement automatic, and found himself committed to a stammered explanation about how tired he was, must get to bed, please forgive; and when he jerked to bolt for the door he actually tripped on the edge of the fender. He fled, casting foolish grins about him, and tried to recover himself outside the door.

Portia had gone upstairs and was on the main landing. He started after her. "I say, Portia—"

She said, "Goodnight."

"Portia, I say, do listen—"

"What is it? I am tired."

"I'm awfully sorry. I won't keep you long. I mean—"

"Well, get on with it," she said, and his heart chilled, for how could he pour out what was in him after this?

"It has been an awfully nice day," he said.

"Really?"

"Oh, Portia, why have you changed?"

"Changed?"

"You've been so nice to me today."

"Have I?"

"Yes, you have." He managed to get one of his stored-up words out. "Adorable."

"Oh! Thank you, kind sir."

"Now you're all—"

"All what?"

"All frowny again."

"Take me as I am. Or not at all."

"I wish I could."

"Could what?"

"Take you—" Her dry, enquiring scrutiny, made him plunge. "To have and to hold. You know. For better or for worse. And all that."

"Do you mean—" Her voice was no warmer— "what you sound as if you mean?"

"I would like us to get married. Really and truly I would. Portia, could you, oh, could you possibly?"

"Whether I could possibly is not the point. I could possibly fly across the English Channel in one of Monsieur Blériot's monoplanes. But I have no intention of doing so."

"Portia, please don't have me on."

"I am not having you on, as you so elegantly put it. What am I to do with a young man who asks for a word or two only when I am about to go to bed, and then calmly proposes?"

"Calmly, oh—"

"Not calmly, it appears."

"Portia, did I offend you when I kissed you? The last time, I mean. You know, when I was—"

"We need not talk about that."

"But I didn't mean to be—"

"My dear Richard, I am not sweet seventeen."

"Sweet seventeen?"

"I have received a considerable part of my education from the servants. I thought all children must have. They have a saying, sweet seventeen and never been kissed."

"Oh, you mean—"

"You are not the first young man who has lost control of himself with me— And apologised, I assure you."

"Oh. But Portia, I do mean it. About wanting to marry you. You see, if you wanted to be left alone—"

"Left alone?"

"You know. At first. I'm sure I could make you love me in time. But I would be happy just to love you. From afar. And cherish you. And give you all the nice times you wanted. Until you were ready—"

"Do I really have to listen to this drivel?"

"Oh!" He gasped for a moment and she stayed to face him, looking as if she enjoyed it.

"*Blow* you," he cried. "You stupid little cat."

He took her shoulders roughly and, as roughly as he had in the afternoon, but more surely, kissed her on the mouth. Then he dropped his hands and stood back from her, breathless, grim and unrepentant.

For another second he could not tell her feelings. Then she smiled. It was one of her 'little' smiles, a fleeting tweak at the corners of her mouth. She said, "Au 'voir, little boy," and disappeared into her room.

Eight

Richard lay on his bed sweating. A cold bath had not
availed. He was inflamed by Portia in her new guise, by
the soft revealed body inside her evening dress. He had
felt it under his hands. A little anger against her lingered
in him together with a heat of triumph at his self-
assertion. He puzzled over her parting words.

Why "au 'voir"? What could she mean? Was it
an invitation?

And then, "little boy". Was that a taunt? A challenge?
What did he know of the world?

All the events of his crowded day went through his
mind. He reviewed again and again the kissing game
of the morning, finding each time some significance in
it. It was Portia who had started it. She had talked
about believing in freedom. She was all for that girl
in F.J.'s novel. She went to tea with a friend who openly
lived with a man.

Then there was Mrs Redington. The more he thought
of her behaviour, the more it bore out F.J.'s assertions
about her. He had been a babe in arms until now.
Grown-up married ladies, even ladies of public repute,
indulged themselves in this business. But all of them?
Surely not all of them. Aunt Marian was so pretty.
Even in her late middle age he thought her pretty. She
had never married. Surely she had not—. He cried
inside his mind, *oh, shut up, shut up, shut up,* and

repeated the prayer which he had silently offered up on many nights during his boyhood, *please, God, stop me thinking terrible wicked things.*

A door was shut upon thoughts of Aunt Marian. But the other thoughts flowed on. It was F.J.'s assumption that Richard, at twenty-two, must surely be as other men, and Richard's pretence-by-acquiescence that he was. It was F.J.'s talk of respectable ladies as if one could get up this sort of game with them as unfailingly as F.J. could get up a game of tennis or billiards. F.J. was not a liar or a boaster. He talked so offhandedly about it. There must be some truth in it.

And what about the talk of the men after dinner? They, too, had taken it all for granted. In his presence, as if it must surely be known to him, they had casually spoken of whole regions that had not existed in his world, regions he saw as dense fetid jungle, in which lurked foulness, fang, infection. Even after three years in Germany he had not known. Even that man of the world, F.J., had implied that Germans and Continentals generally were given to that sort of thing. It was comic enough to think of foreigners loose in their morals and presumably therefore ranking below clean, sturdy England, Queen of the World; a belief professed every day in speeches and articles by eminent Englishmen. But some such idiocy must have cut him off from perceiving reality during his time in Germany.

He had taken for granted that some men were rotters and some women were fallen. That was standard Victorian belief. As a modern young man he had also understood that a certain number of respectable people occasionally ignored the imperative of matrimony. He upheld their right to do so. But even in advanced novels

the couples who "did" always had some moral justification.

He had read much and he was greatly influenced by
the novelists he revered. There was F.J. himself. There
was Mr Forster, who in his calm, sweet way condemned
abnegation as a refusal of life and praised young men
who rejoiced in the enjoyment of their powers. Still, all
the people in Mr Forster's novels, even his passionate
Italians, behaved, in their various modes, with decency.

All this was in Richard's mind; not as a train of
thought but as a turmoil of thoughts. Kissing, "I believe
in freedom", fingers on his knee, F.J. and his respectable
ladies, the novels he had read, men round a table after
dinner grunting about baronesses, little girls, dukes,
bishops and unspeakable contortions, churned in his
mind, and with them mingled too much alcohol in his
blood, the effects of too much rich food, too much
excitement, even the too-much-vainglory of having
spoken out at last to Portia.

There arose in his veins a congestion as if the blood
were forcing its way to his brain like mercury in a
thermometer. Fool, fool, fool! Quadruple and quintuple
fool that he was! The other men treated him as a man
like themselves but he was not. And Portia – Au 'voir,
little boy." It was a taunt and an invitation.

For how many years, since his 'teens, had he resisted
the demand of his body? How many times had he
suffered pain of body and mind? And to be laughed at
for it! Yes, *she* was laughing at him. Clearly she did
as the world did. He alone, fool, fool, fool, did not. She
had laughed at him and tossed him a final, testing
invitation. Call it an ultimatum.

It was that night of last January all over again. That

had come to nothing. This must not. He got out of bed and put on dressing-gown and slippers. He moved like a sleep-walker, or like a mechanical creature. His mind remained stunned except for certain simple commands that went through it like the strips of message on a telegram. It was like that January night even to the fact that his real intent, raging in his body, was refused entry to his mind, in which he heard alone the self-deceiving injunction, "I must talk to her. Simply talk to her."

He crept along his corridor and down the narrow stairs, fearful of every creak. He stepped through the little door on to the main landing. From the great stair window facing him poured a pale radiance of moonlight that revealed every object more starkly than electricity.

He stood at Portia's door. He raised his clenched hand to knock then feared that she might come to the door and send him away. He could not risk a whispered altercation on the landing. Better to tiptoe silently into the room and gently awaken her.

He opened the door cautiously. It groaned. Moonlight streamed past him into the room. He saw Portia. She sat up in bed and looked at him. She was not alone.

The man next to her sat up, too. It was F.J.

Richard could not move. Neither Portia nor F.J. looked dismayed. Portia glared at Richard. F.J. sighed, and cleared his nostrils with a long sniff. Portia said, "Get out."

Richard said, "I'm sorry."

He shut the door and went back to bed. He felt nothing at all. He lay down to indulge in perplexities and sorrows. He stayed awake for a long time but he was calm.

Nine

Next morning the shrilling of birds announced another day of the relentless fine weather, but although there were the usual early noises from the servants' quarters most of the gentlefolk at Ashtons slept late. It was Sunday. An exception was Miss Snell, who went for her usual walk. Another was F.J. He was up early, shaving and reflecting upon the events of last night.

It was all a damn nuisance. No question now of a second night with her. Richard apart, she was not his sort. He thought more about the girl than about the boy. Young Richard was all right. One might have foreseen the farce. Richard was besotted by the bitch. Poor lad, boys like that always fell in love with the cold bitches. And cold she was. Young Latt was not the sort to talk. He only needed a little kindness.

But he, F. J. Dobbs, was after all Someone. To have been caught in bed was – it was belittling.

As to her, he wondered, as he had so often before, why he kept on getting mixed up with little baggages whose passions were all in the head. Well, he never could keep away from a willing one. And he had known she was willing from the start.

Come to that, he never could forgo the adventure of what he called "the midnight creep". Sordid it might be, but he always felt a childish tickle of adventure when, in a strange house, after tossing an imaginary coin, he toptoed to a strange bedroom uninvited. So far he had never guessed wrong.

There had been some consequences. One father had made an unfulfilled threat to horsewhip him. Another father had gone about the clubs making querulous accusations about F.J. It so happened that the father in question was himself a notable lecher, and only succeeded in arousing a spate of jokes about the town at his own expense, F.J. coming off in consequence as a sort of Don Juanish hero.

In short, F.J.'s little adventures had made him the subject of a certain amount of scandalised gossip among people who liked to think themselves in the know, which was much to the benefit of a writer, but not of open scandal, which would have been ruinous.

Still, it was a tricky plank to walk. Nothing would ever stop him from walking it whenever he saw a signal from the other side.

This was how it went when he appeared at Portia's bedside. Portia sat up and said, "Oh! Mr Dobbs."

"All right, my girl," were his first words. "No more nonsense. I want you."

"Indeed?"

"I think you want me," he said more gently, and tried his sad smile on her.

"What makes you think that?"

"I know," he said, as gently. He let his dressing-gown drop off and stood naked by the bed. She looked intently at him, with no other visible feeling than that of fascination at the sight of this small, white, paunchy male body; remaining quite still and unmoved as the body in turn rapidly showed signs of violent interest in her.

"I suppose if I screamed," she said as he turned back the cover, "there would be a dreadful to-do."

"You won't," he said, getting into bed. "What you want to hear is how not to have a baby."

"Oh? How?"

He made this matter clear to her. "You're a virgin, of course," he said.

"Why of course?"

"I'm not one of your young fools. Listen, my pet. It could be quite nasty with someone else. I shall make it rather nice."

"I should hope so."

"Take off your nightdress, please. I hate fumbling under nightdresses."

"I would not incommode you for worlds."

"Stop talking like Jane Austen, my dear." She pulled her nightdress over her head. "You look charming, little Portia."

"That is the first nice thing you have said. I thought you were supposed to say nice things all the time."

"I shall do them instead. Now lie back."

"If you will stop talking like a doctor," she said. His hands pressed her gently back. A moment later she said, quietly, "Oh," and she made no further significant sound.

He had found her to be willing, co-operative, teach-able in an earnest but uninspired way; but with no natural talent, spontaneity, eagerness or sense of harmony. Also she showed no signs of love, hero-worship or gratitude, gifts which many other girls had brought him together with that of their persons. He decided that although she was a lucky find during a dull weekend (which reminded him, he hadn't yet had a chance to talk alone with Ralph Menant about the stock market) she was a cold little piece. She was cold in mind as well as body. One of those virgins who were hardly worth the bother.

They lay side by side, relaxed. "Well," he said, "now you have had your first lover. Was it nice?"

"Do you doubt it?"

"I like to hear."

"You mean it is polite to say thank you?"

"You're a prickly one. It's the best thing about you."

"Oh? Is that to say that in other things I have been found wanting?"

"My dear girl, you've been delightful."

"That came rather glibly."

"What do you expect, my love? A declamation from *Romeo and Juliet*?"

"I know the difference between F. J. Dobbs and Shakespeare."

"You're quite a little mistress of ambiguities."

"I am sorry. I suppose I should have said it was nice. You *were* very nice to me."

"You suppose? I know *I* was nice. What about *it*?"

"To be quite truthful, I don't really know."

"First time. It's natural. In a few minutes more you will know better." During this interlude he had, from time to time, leaned down to kiss her in one way or another, and his hands moved in tentative caresses. He felt as little response as he had the first time.

"Why a few minutes?" she said. "Why not now?"

"If you said that out of eagerness I'd be happy. Unfortunately you put the question like a student at a science class."

"I'm sorry."

"It takes time," he said, "because I am not the young man I was, and because I would like to feel some response from you. Don't you feel anything?"

"Yes. Your hands. It is pleasant. Do go on."

"My lamb, you positively quench me. Is there nothing that draws you to *me*?"

"Such as what? If you tell me, I shall do my best."

"My dear girl—" He desisted and lay back. "Never mind, it's all a matter of temperament."

She said, "Talking of mistresses—"

"Who was?"

"You said I was a mistress of ambiguities. —You have got a lot of mistresses, haven't you?"

"Don't listen to gossip."

"You have, haven't you?"

"I have a wife, the mother of my children. I love her and I love them. And because man is a complex, confused sort of beast, I also have mistresses. One at a time. My present mistress is an artist of great accomplishment. She satisfies needs of my mind and spirit in certain ways in which my wife, alas, cannot. In other regions of myself my wife remains paramount."

"I understand," Portia said. "But am I not now your mistress?"

He sat up abruptly. "My mistress? Listen to me, my love—"

"But after what has taken place—"

"Oh, come off it, lovey. Don't play the Victorian miss."

She spoke stiffly. "I was speaking technically. In that sense, surely—"

"We shall have a delightful weekend. And then we shall go our own ways."

"I see."

"Of course you do. And I'm sure we shall always be the best of friends."

"As I expect you are with all your girls."

"Exactly." F.J. spoke with great firmness. He had experienced this "mistress" talk from casual girls before. It threatened tears, letters, claims, silly creatures going about claiming an unwarranted status. He always stamped hard on it. "And I knew you would see, as you have seen. You are young, modern, clear-eyed, civilised. You are fit to be the heroine of one of my books, intelligent, unafraid, demanding freedom for yourself and scorning to make claims upon a man's freedom."

"It's nice to know I'm all that," Portia said.

"A jolly time and then – friends forever."

He leaned down to kiss her and discovered to his great relief that he was sufficiently recovered to bestow upon her the delights he had promised. At this moment the door opened. He sat up once more. Richard Latt stood gaping at them in a spread of pale moonlight.

Portia, too, was awake, drowsily reviewing the events of the night in a bed once more unshared. There was a stained sheet she supposed the servants would notice. Servants noticed and knew everything as she knew well, having, in her days as a little pitcher with big ears, learned much from them. She did not care.

Her problem was what to do next. Particularly it applied to her conduct when she went downstairs. In general it concerned her whole mode of life.

She did not, to start with, know what course to take in future about this sex business. She had not been revolted, and she had noted a certain limited amount of pleasure, but she felt some disenchantment about it. It was a small repayment to receive for a lot of activity that seemed to her undignified with all those heavings about and Heaven knew what, and in the bargain having another person's weight on top of her. And F.J., she was sure, must be as good a practitioner as any. Had not he himself told her that most men were much worse? She had not, therefore, derived from last night any great inclination towards the pastime. On the other hand (and this was the problem) what concerned her was not her appetites but her social stance.

(She put, for the moment, Richard out of her mind. There were more important things to settle.)

On the one hand, being emancipated about sex meant (as a Suffragette friend of hers, who had a way of kissing her too affectionately, had warned her) allowing unwarrantable intrusions into one's privacy; on the other hand, one did want to be emancipated, and to be seen to be emancipated. One did not want to be known as a shrinking violet. She had no notion, in general, of what to do with herself. Her one defined aspiration was to be up-to-date.

Several of her friends had, or had professed to have, love affairs "in the fullest sense of the word" – they always explained things in such delicate phrases, and never with the chuckles and gross words that F.J. had used to enlighten her last night. She would, at least, have one to talk about.

It was her one positive gain from the episode. She smarted, when she let herself dwell on it, at F.J.'s rebuff. She well understood the meaning of his sharp and instant reproof concerning the matter of being his mistress, and was not the girl to be taken in by the insulting flattery in which he had coated it. It had come as a blow, for during the act her mind had been far away, spinning scenes in which she appeared as his mistress, sometimes accompanying him on exotic travels or meeting the great and glamorous at his side, sometimes appearing alone, but aware of people whispering, furtively pointing her out. "See that girl? The beautiful blonde girl over there. That's F.J.'s mistress."

And she did so want something to fill her life, which bored her and was without meaning. She sometimes thought of work, but she was too lazy. How cosy it was, now, to curl up in bed as long as she wanted to! She could not get up at the same early hour every morning and go, perhaps in some crowded public conveyance, to the same place to perform the same task, to have to do what some other person told her, and remain there for a fixed number of hours. Some of her friends did it and called it freedom. She thought it was frightful.

Nor did she know what her father would say if she had proposed to work for money. He was a Liberal and easy-going about advanced tendencies, but he was trying hard to establish himself among the old landowning families roundabout, and sometimes he could at a stroke become sternly old-fashioned, declaring (Mrs Menant often provoked him to such pronouncements) that they had a position to maintain.

Her mother, too, was a treacherous ally. Mrs Menant preached every form of progress, but practised few. She wrote "advanced" novels but cut acquaintances who lived by the precepts advocated in her tales. She contributed articles to the journals of the respectable wing of the Women's Suffrage movement but thought the Suffragettes were vulgar. She called herself a socialist but she had never marched in a procession. Not that Portia had given any practical expression to her emancipated views, either; but Portia's inaction arose from laziness, and from the notion that doing anything was rather absurd.

No-one was more quickly outraged by any practical departure from convention than Mrs Menant. Portia knew how her mother would have, triumphantly, "solved" the problem of finding work for Portia – she would have made Portia her secretary, and the notion of being for any length of time close to her mother filled Portia with loathing. She cared, in an idle way, for her father, but she could not abide her mother. She had to come home for weekends, but she meant to go on staying as long as she could with the amiable Marian Holland.

And then, on Friday night, standing in front of F.J. in the drawing-room with the silver bowl in her hands, she had looked at him and he had looked up at her. It had only been for a couple of seconds, but a bolt of excitement had gone through her, a greater excitement than she had subsequently experienced in bed. She had felt for the moment helpless, between the paws of a predator, unwilling, repelled by his pudgy face and paunch and squeaky voice yet with curiosity crawling all over her skin to know what he, the first bold male ever to look her in the eyes, was like; and so it had gone when she awoke to find him at her bedside.

She retained one gain from the night's events. F.J. could not take it away from her. She could boast; only, of course, to a select circle of girl friends, and perhaps only in tantalising hints. All the same, it was something to be able to let fall that she had gone in for *it* and, immensely more promising, that she had a relationship with the great F.J. Dobbs. Oh, he and she had agreed to keep it secret. (She was elaborating versions of the tale already.) His wife, poor woman, he loves her, but – he has other needs, spiritual and intellectual, which she simply cannot satisfy. He calls me his true comrade—

Checking these fantasies was a streak of plain old-fashioned prudence. Was it wise to boast? She wondered if it would really, in these advanced times, spoil her chances of matrimony if she were known to be no longer *virgo intacta*. For in time she must, she supposed, get married. She did not hunger for any of its aspects – the bed, the children, the housekeeping – but there was the matter of status.

Most of her friends would marry, and they would score points, so to speak, according to the wealth, position or other boastworthinesses of their husbands. Spinsters were a little ridiculous, unless they were formidable and brainy like Miss Snell, which Portia knew she was not.

So she came to the question of Richard.

The effect of his appearance had only been to cause one big heartbeat of fright. After that, to her own surprise, she had felt herself positively gloating at him in triumph. His face! Of course, she had looked daggers at him.

She knew (and F.J. had told her) that Richard would not blab. He would have taken it too much to heart; and he was simply not the sort. Indeed, F.J. had said, "Be nice to the lad."

How, then, was she to treat him when they came face to face?

Her mind drifted away from this question and she found herself considering him as a general prospect. As in fact, a catch. (Though she despised this word as cheap, for surely a girl should not have to catch a man; the men strove for her and she made her choice.) What? – who? – was she likely to get?

The young men of her circle were all moderately clever, all either a little too earnest or too doggedly witty, all engaged in some profession, all with a little money coming to them but none with much. None of them was inspiring. Of course she despised money but it had a certain importance, since she required a certain modest luxury. Father would provide, of course, but she was one of three daughters, and the other two would probably produce numerous progeny.

She did not fancy any of her father's City gents, although a few had shown signs of being ready to offer themselves, and with a lot of money in the bargain. "Never be an old man's darling" had been one of the adages she had learned from her mentors below stairs.

What she would have adored was an alliance with a handsome, brilliant and enormously wealthy sprig of the aristocracy; for instance, one of those young men of the circle known as The Souls, whose attainments were celebrated in serious magazines and whose revels were reported in the cheaper newspapers. These were, alas, beyond her ken and might remain so. Mrs Menant could get Mr Asquith to the house, at least for a luncheon cut short by the excuse of other engagements, but not his golden sons.

Which brought her back to the question of Richard.

He really was an impossible, clumsy ass, barging in on her like that. But the fact that he was such a lunatic about her would make him easy to handle.

He was no Apollo but he was not repulsive.

He had shown some unexpected spurts of intelligence this weekend.

Clumsy? Oh, yes, but he might be made a sort of human pony, eager to eat out of her hand, and she would be free, to be advanced, to hold court, to enjoy more exciting company – the handsome, the glamorous, perhaps, in time, the great. In short, her due.

He had, according to Father, a fair amount of money (in trust for the moment) from his parents and of course he would get everything from Marian Holland when she died, and *she* was not badly off. With father's contribution added, it would not make for a bad life.

The points mounted in Richard's favour. There was no question of committing herself. But until her life took some decisive turn it was a pity to let him slip away.

She still could not decide how to proceed with him, but she knew how to make a start. Dressing, she chose her outfit with particular care, and she took a lot of time doing her hair.

Richard slept heavily. He had not gone to sleep until the edges of the curtains had been rimmed white with daylight. He awoke when the maid knocked at the door with the hot-water can, grunted something to her and drifted back into a half-sleep.

His mind was awake, although sluggish. He realised that he was trying to prolong this state of half-awareness. There was refuge in it, and in bodily warmth. With awakening had come the instant memory of his problems, and he did not want to confront them.

He could not stop the fog of sleep from clearing, nor his mind from working. He felt nothing more than a heavy, woeful perplexity. He had no animus against

Portia. She hardly came into his thoughts. About F.J. he could not make up his mind. He could not hate the man, but slashes of resentment went through him against someone so much older, so much more experienced, who so easily could take everything from him. It was the resentment of a child, knowing his own lack of resource, against the seemingly omnipotent, omnipossessive grown-up. His hopeful illusions had been wiped away – not about F.J.'s character, but about the friendship he had imagined with such pride to be germinating between them this weekend. All gone.

All gone, too, his briefly-born germ of confidence in himself. It was plain, he told himself, obvious, incontrovertible, that Portia had been F.J.'s mistress for a long time. Perhaps everyone knew about it but Richard Latt. His belief in his own foolish ignorance threatened to expand to infinity. He remembered all those walks in London when he had talked doggedly on about this or that topic, about anything but his own true thoughts and feelings. What a bore he must have been! What a callow fool in contrast with the great man whose comments on life were hers to enjoy. He was all the more sure that life as he had until now imagined it was an untrue, child's fairy-tale. Real life was something different altogether. Everybody but Richard Latt knew about it. The men after dinner talked about it. Portia lived it. The whole species but himself; he was excluded. Everybody must laugh at him, even if some of them did so sympathetically. How else was he to account for Portia's behaviour towards him yesterday? The kisses, the bright smiles, the confidences, her fervour in his support. She could only have been playing with him. Oh, cruel girl!

His wish was to stay in bed all day; or until some time

when the house was empty and he could pack his bag and, unseen by anyone, creep away.

Instead he got up and went to the window. Long drifts of cloud gathered over Long Down, their white lumpy topsides dappled with shadow, their undersides dark grey. Blue sky showed in irregular channels between the clouds but no sunshine gilded the morning. The green of the hillside was dull.

The lump in his breast was one of determination. As well that it was a dull day, for it was Sunday and he must wear the formal suit he had packed. He shaved, washed and brushed the springy fair hanks of his hair down assiduously until they made a smooth helmet. He took his clothes from the wardrobe, brushed and pressed by the servants, and his black shoes, their toecaps gleaming. He had no idea how to face either of them. He could form no plan. But he dressed punctiliously, in crisp new shirt, high collar, dark tie, waistcoat, high narrow trousers and high-lapelled jacket. He inspected himself like a soldier in the mirror, found nothing at fault and went bravely downstairs to breakfast.

Ten

Richard felt his heart racing when he went into the
morning room, but only Miss Snell was there – for the
two maids standing one at each end of the sideboard
were no more to be noticed than if they had been hat-
stands.

"Good morning, Miss Snell."

"Good morning, Mr Latt."

He looked unhappily at the array of dishes. He took a
spoonful of scrambled eggs. He went to sit opposite Miss
Snell. She said, "I see you do not favour the large
breakfast."

He put a fragment to his lips but he could hardly
bear to eat it. "No."

"Nor I. A slice of toast and honey, that is my rule."

"Yes— Indeed?"

"At home I buy honey of Hymettus. I confess that it
tastes no different from any other good honey but the
classical reference pleases me."

"Yes. I'm sure."

"A spoonful of egg contains quite enough protein to
sustain you for the morning."

"Indeed?"

"I eat sparely but with discrimination. And I am, as
is often observed, an energetic woman. I am none the
worse."

"No."

"Men guzzle disgustingly. I am glad to see that you are an exception." He managed to affect a smile. "Every man in England who earns a decent week's wage or more stuffs himself like a hog. In consequence he may well die of apoplexy. The very poor die of many other things but they do not drop like flies with apoplexy." He was trying to force some comment from himself when she added, "But I dare say I am only confirming your opinion of me as a crank—"

"Oh, no, Miss Snell—"

"Then what shall we talk about?"

The cold yellow lumps of egg on his plate nauseated him. They provided no inspiration. "The – ah, the weather," he said. "It's – ah, changing, is it not?"

"One cannot say yet. When I was out walking this morning—"

"You have been out?"

"Oh, yes, from six o'clock. I walked over the Downs to Alfriston, followed the Cuckmere north and returned along the main road. The wind was south-westerly when I started out. That is the prevailing wind in this region. But it has been backing round ever since. It does, you know—"

"And in what quarter does it stand now?" F.J. was in the doorway. Richard's insides chilled. F.J. came in. "Good morning, Miss Snell. Good morning, young man—" He dropped a hand for a moment on Richard's shoulder.

"It is blowing the cloud out to sea," Miss Snell said. "As so often, it has veered right round to the opposite quarter."

"And have we seen the end of this extraordinary heat wave?"

"Possibly."

F.J. peered absorbedly along the sideboard. "I hope not. At least for one more day. We have our cricket tomorrow. Have we not, young Richard?"

Richard muttered, "Yes."

F.J. addressed the maid at the far end of the sideboard. "Ham, my dear. Cut it thick. Plenty of fat— That's right— I'll need more than that—" To the other maid, "Three of those." He let her scoop three fried eggs on to his plate. "And I think some crispy bacon will if anything enhance the ham." He waited while his plate was piled with meat.

Miss Snell said, "I have been telling Mr Latt why so many prosperous men die of apoplexy."

F.J. turned and sat next to Richard. To the young man it seemed as if blow upon blow were being dealt to his heart. "Over-eating," F.J. said. "You're quite right. I saw that as soon as I began to study science. But until that time I'd eaten too little. What would you? Eh, Richard?" Richard did not answer. F.J. said, "Not much on your plate, my lad."

"I'm not very hungry."

F.J. cocked his head and for a moment the heavy lids of his eyes lifted to reveal a concerned scrutiny. He said, "You'll have to feed better than that tomorrow if you're to hit any sixes."

The Argents came in. Greetings were exchanged and the weather discussed. The Argents went to the sideboard and surveyed the food, with a twittering as of birds.

"You haven't told us your strong points as a cricketer," F.J. said to Richard. "Are you a slogger? A demon bowler? Or a stonewaller?"

"I—"

Portia came in. She wore a simple costume : a jacket over a blouse, with matching skirt, white linen with a blue stripe. Richard ached with tenderness for her. Her face was composed. She sat down next to Miss Snell, on the far side from Richard and a little way down the table. She said to the nearer maid, "Tea. And toast. And more tea for Miss Snell. And Mr Dobbs. Richard, would you like some more tea?"

Richard could not look up from his plate. "No, thank you."

"Mother takes tea in her room on Sunday morning—" She was addressing the gathering in general. "Father has had breakfast and is busy in the stables. He will join us soon. And how are you enjoying the country, Miss Snell?"

"As always, immensely."

"I would like to start another course of lectures next term. Have you any at your college that would interest me?"

"Have you considered working for one of the London University degrees?"

"I might well do. Inform me, Miss Snell."

"I take it you have matriculated."

"I have the Cambridge Higher Local Certificate."

The two women went into conference. The Argents were eating as if engaged in private prayer. F.J. leaned to Richard and spoke low. "Young Richard, I want a word with you."

"Yes, sir."

"After. Eh?"

Miss Snell said, "I think you had better come to the college when we are both back in London. You may then judge us, and I shall judge you. And now tell me, young lady, do you take much exercise when you are in town?"

"Only walking."

"Real walking? Or young-lady-like strolls?"

Portia looked across to Richard with the brightest of smiles. "Which would you say, Richard? Richard is my companion when I walk in London."

He said curtly, "We walk in the Park."

"Not strenuously, I'm afraid," Portia said. "Miss Snell has us there, Richard."

"Yes."

"*Mens sana in corpore sano*," said Miss Snell. "Such sayings are the most trite because they are the most true."

"Without a doubt," Portia said. "We must do better in future, don't you think, Richard?"

"I say—" F.J. raised a loud and squeaky voice as if he had been left in the background long enough. "What about a walk after breakfast?"

Mr Argent lifted an ascetic face from his nibblings. "Mrs Argent and I are going to church with Mr Menant. Mrs Menant, I understand, is indisposed."

"Not at all," Portia said. "Mother doesn't hold with it."

"Then what about a walk for non-churchgoers?" F.J. said.

"I am a Unitarian," Miss Snell said. "A lax one, too, I must confess. This morning I shall be glad to treat the Downs as my cathedral and pay my tribute to the beneficent deity in the fresh air."

"Bravo," F.J. said, "it shall be a gentle and reverential walk. Portia?"

"I shall see."

"Of course," he said gravely. "Of course. We shall

have the Redingtons, because *he* wants to buttonhole me about a conference on sweated labour he is getting up. Richard, you must come."

Richard rose from his chair. "I must get ready for church."

"You are ready for church."

Richard went out of the room without answering. He was at the foot of the stairs when F.J. came out after him. "My boy— Come in here."

Richard let himself be ushered into the drawing-room. A maid was there, dusting. "Be off with you," F.J. said. When she had closed the door behind her, he said, "You had a shock last night, didn't you?"

Richard was silent.

"I am tempted to talk like the hearty Miss Snell and invite you to take it like a man."

Richard kept his silence. F.J. said, "I am sorry."

Surprise forced Richard to speak. "Sorry?"

"I would not have hurt your feelings for worlds." There was nothing Richard could say. F.J. went on, "What was of small account to me was enormous – heartbreaking – to you."

Richard's response was a gaze so piteously questioning that F.J. added, "You wonder how I can say 'of small account'."

Richard cried, "How can you talk like that of her?" It was F.J.'s turn to remain silent. In a lowered voice, Richard said, "I never would have – I didn't know—"

"There was nothing to know before last night. I never knew the girl before. I shan't see her again. Last night was the start and finish of it. The fault was all mine. You will understand one day."

"Excuse me." Richard hurried out of the room.

"No, no," Mr Argent said, "I am not distressed. A gentle walk will do me no harm."

He had paused, with his wife, Mr Menant and Richard, at a bend in the lane which led up from Ashtons to the village. The two older men wore morning coats and toppers. Richard wore a bowler.

"I feel responsible for you," Mr Menant said. It was Borrett the chauffeur's day off but Mr Menant had offered to drive the party to church. The Argents had turned out to be old-fashioned Sabbatarians and had insisted on walking in spite of Mr Argent's invalid state.

"If we walk slowly and pause often I shall not suffer greatly," Mr Argent said.

"Let us walk very slowly then and pause very often. There is a path a little way on. We can miss the worst of this lane."

"Would that I could attend the House tomorrow."

"The debate? Surely you have no worries about the result."

"My voice ought to be heard. But the doctors forbid." He looked out across the hillside that fell away from the lane. Ashtons and its gardens lay in full view. "A beautiful sight."

"I bought it eight years ago. It cost me nine thousand pounds, with a trout stream and thirty-one acres."

They moved on slowly. Above them on the other side of the lane the woods massed. Here and there the garden fence and gate of a keeper's cottage were let into the high bank. "Just another bend and we can leave the lane," Mr Menant said.

They paused again. Mr Menant went on, "I've bought farms when I could. I enjoy running an estate. I run one farm myself for the home and let the rest. Low rents. Improvement loans. I do my best for the tenants."

Mr Argent said, "If all employers were like you! We should have socialism."

"Come," Mr Menant said. "I read some of you fellows. I am a capitalist. Since the labour of workmen produces all wealth according to your chaps, I am robbing them however well I treat them."

"You refer to the dogmatists," Mr Argent said, "the materialists. They have no future. Man does not live by bread alone."

"Quite so. But I don't think we can expect workmen to put the spirit first when the well-off don't. Do you know, I should like to become established in the county. I would like to give up the office eventually. I have good men to run it. I could be happy making this my whole life. The Bench. County committees. That sort of thing. I should like to get on better with my neighbours, though. I'm afraid some of them still think it treason to house men better than horses. And I've rebuilt most of my cottages. Given them running water."

"Admirable."

"I wonder if they think so. They are amiable enough. Some of them come to dine and ask me back. But I can't help suspecting that although I'm a Liberal they think me a rank Socialist for giving my keepers good wages. I protest to them that it pays. I make a better profit out of my land than any of them. That's the argument for good conditions. But I don't think they believe in profits. And I dare say I'm still a bit of an intruder after only nine years. One must be patient in the countryside."

They walked on. A small boy came round the bend in the road. He wore his Sunday best grey Norfolk jacket and breeches. He had a strip of surgical tape from top to bottom of his right cheek. Mr Menant said, "Why, it's Charlie Grayle! Come here, Charlie."

The boy trotted across and stood as if at attention in front of him. Richard had been walking behind the others. He came up and looked at the boy. "Hallo! You're the boy we knocked down. How are you?"

"All right, sir."

"Of course he is," Mr Menant said. He turned to the Argents. "A little mishap with our car last Wednesday. My wife called the next day to see how he was and he was climbing trees. Weren't you, young Charlie?"

"Yes, sir."

"Now, you listen to me, my little lad. Next time you come through that hedge, stop first and look."

"Yes, sir."

Richard looked about him and realised for the first time that they were at the scene of the accident. Mr Menant gave the boy a sixpence and dismissed him. Where the bank dropped away a path led through the woods; the short cut. He opened the gate and ushered the Argents through.

Richard did not follow. He looked for a long time at the road, taking in the picture of the bend. He walked uphill and looked all round the projecting bank. He saw the red board with PRIVATE on it nailed to the overhanging tree.

He stood in the middle of the road, remembering. It all tallied. He was sure now. It corresponded exactly to the picture he had seen before the accident ever happened. It was no use pretending to himself any more that it was a deception of memory.

"Richard!" Mr Menant's voice came from among the trees.

"Coming, sir." He went to catch up with them.

> O God, our help in ages past,
> Our hope for years to come,
> Our shelter from the stormy blast,
> And our eternal home.

The church was large, light and airy. There was a great deal of new stone, new brass, new woodwork. It had been much restored in the last century. Plates of brass or white marble in the walls proclaimed the virtues of past squires and their ladies, officers on land and sea, the deeds of local gentlemen fallen in battles from Quebec to Magersfontein. The hymn rang in the rafters. The church was full. The gentry were in their pews. The rest looked to be doctor, estate agent, lawyer and such, and the clerks and shopkeepers, and all their families, and that numerous village class, unmarried single ladies with small private incomes.

> A thousand ages in Thy sight
> Are like an evening gone,
> Short as the watch that ends the night
> Before the rising sun.

The greetings to Mr Menant when he came into church had all seemed friendly enough. Richard tried to direct his thoughts to Mr Menant and his ambitions. Sir Ralph Menant. Perhaps he aimed higher than simple acceptance. His thoughts would not stay on Mr Menant. He sought relief from his own phantoms by singing heartily. He lifted up his face to gaze at the vicar, an old man with a bloodhound face and a few hanks of silver hair.

> Time, like an ever-rolling stream,
> Bears all its sons away;
> They fly forgotten, as a dream
> Dies at the opening day.

But Richard could not stop his thoughts from flying to one terrible fact. He had foreseen precisely the accident of last Wednesday.

This revelation had taken possession of him. He could not even fix his mind on the events of last night or on his encounter this morning with Portia and F.J. He told himself that he was confronted with a mystery. It was blank and impenetrable as the hardened steel hull of a Dreadnought. No use banging his head against it. He tried to listen to the sermon.

The text had escaped his attention but it seemed that the sermon had something to do with the significance of the Sacraments. The vicar stood in the pulpit ignoring his congregation, peering closely at a sheaf of papers. ". . . according to the Tridentine definition, all Sacraments were instituted by Our Lord Jesus Christ . . ."

Why had Portia been so kind to him at breakfast? It leaped into his mind. She had looked so simple and fresh and beautiful. It was not her fault. F.J. had admitted as much. She must have been trying to tell him so herself, when she spoke so gently and brightly to him. If he, Richard, felt so helpless and inexperienced in face of this old and famous man, how helpless and inexperienced must Portia have been! Poor girl, she must have been clay in F.J.'s hands.

She must be seeking his – yes, his, Richard's – forgiveness. Dear, silly girl! What was there to forgive? Did she think he could not understand how it had all come about? – how a girl like her would be dazzled, mesmerised, yes, terrified, by this man so sure of himself and his power?

". . . Thomas Aquinas carefully distinguishes between the Divine Nature, which is the source of grace, and the humanity of Our Lord, by which the gift is mediated to us. . ." From all parts of the church came shufflings, coughs, whispering. Richard was not the only one who could not keep his mind on the sermon. His thoughts started off on a new tack and now he saw Portia in a quite different way. All his previous experiences of her fitted together like the bits of a jigsaw puzzle and he saw a new picture. She was selfish, callous, bored, idle and empty. She was an inveterate schemer. She could pick up and discard people like cards in a game to suit her changing needs. She was trying to make use of him in some way after last night's imbroglio. Perhaps she was trying to ensure his silence. Perhaps she had even been put up to it by F.J.

". . . a Sacrament being a sensible sign of grace, it is obvious that something visible or audible or tangible is requisite . . ."

Two pictures of Portia. Here was a mystery, too. It was a lot for a young man to bear, a young man who had just discovered how little he knew of life.

And in a blink his thoughts were disrupted once more. He was looking at one of his pictures. It was The Man In The Mud. He saw it against the bright white daylight of the tall windows behind the altar. There it was, a clear composed picture yet transparent – the sea of mud, the pools of gleaming water, the wilderness of rusty fanged wire, the dead man looking little more than a crumpled uniform flung upon the wire with a head and limbs protruding.

It was there. It was gone. But it left in its place a question. If the picture of The Child's Accident had been a foresight, what was this one? What were all the others?

The vicar was working to some kind of conclusion. ". . . the scriptural ideal of marriage has been the cement of the Christian world and has been a mighty influence for the sanctification of family life and the development of character. Who would contemplate for a moment. . .?"

Richard muttered, "I'm sorry," to Mr Menant, and tiptoed out of the church.

There at the gate was Borrett, with the Daimler. Richard went to him. "What are you doing here?"

"Mr Menant asked me. Just to take the old gentleman back to Ashtons. Mr Argent."

"He's very thoughtful," Richard said. "Mr Argent is a heart case— Borrett, you've read Mr Dobbs' novels?"

"Yes, sir."

"The science stories?"

"Every one, sir."

"Do you ever read serious science?"

"What I can understand of it."

"Do you think science can really see any way of reaching through time?"

"You're thinking of that Time Voyager story."

"No, let's just say – seeing through time. Seeing the future."

"Seeing—? Well, sir, science tells us that anything is possible—"

"Yes—"

"But if you ask me—"

"Well, Borrett?"

"I've got a young lady, sir. As a matter of fact she's waiting for me now. She lives down the street—"

"Yes, Borrett?"

"There's one thing I can't stand with her. Take her to a fair and she's into a booth asking what's in the crystal ball. Or I'm in her house and some old Romany hag comes to the street door. Straightway Violet's asking me for a penny to have her palm read. I can't walk in there without she's getting her mother to read the tea-leaves. It wouldn't be that sort of thing you mean?"

"Not exactly."

Borrett said, "I'll tell you one thing. The future's a closed book and it's the one thing we've got to be thankful for. One minute you're happy. The next – it would give me grey hairs to know. Live for today, I say, and let the future alone. Eh, sir?"

"Yes."

Mr Menant and the Argents came out of church. The Argents had no objection to going back on wheels. Richard explained that he didn't feel well and Mr Menant was concerned because Richard had excused himself from luncheon yesterday for the same reason. "Jump in," he said. "We'll get you home and you can rest."

"Oh, no, sir. I'd rather walk. I need the air."

By dint of insisting, Richard at last found himself alone in the churchyard.

*   *   *

135

The churchyard was on the brow of the ridge. From it, Ashtons was an E-shaped doll's-house amid a patchwork quilt of fields. Richard turned away from the prospect and wandered among the weathered tombstones, many of them so old that they had sunk to crazy angles, their inscriptions defaced by the salt Channel gales or the erosions of lichen.

He stopped at a large tomb surmounted by an urn.

The remains of
MARY HENRIETTA GOOD
She combined with the
most Elegant Simplicity
of Person the Purest
Taste as a Singer. She
Gladdened Life by the
Charm of her Manner

Taken from this Life in
her 21st Year, 2nd August
1806

It was calming to think about Mary Henrietta Good, the singer of purest taste, and to wonder who her eulogist had been. All was settled for her, poor dear, and for all these others in this graveyard.

"India is a graveyard for children." He heard the voice clearly. It was his father's. He often heard it. Oh, it was settled for his father and mother, too, lying beneath their headstones in a cemetery in India. Skulls and bones they were, like those beneath these stained grey stones.

He had lain in his bed, five years old, and through the thin partition in the bungalow he had heard:

His mother: "I can't bear to part with him."

His father: "My darling, India is a graveyard for children. He must go home to Marian."

Marian was his mother's sister. He remembered his parents as sharply as if he had left them yesterday. His father was tall – immensely tall to a small child – with fair hair like Richard's but in a tousled thatch. He had a thin, drooping, humorous moustache which went with his smile. He was always smiling, he had a joke ready every time he saw his little son. He always had time for his little boy. He always had something new to teach him. The little boy climbed up his father, sat astride his shoulders, shrieked with joy when his father swung him round and round—Mother was dark and pretty. She looked like Aunt Marian. She was not ashamed to hug and kiss her little boy fifty times a day. They were ageless in his mind but how young they had died! His father had been twenty-eight, his mother twenty-seven, when the epidemic had killed them.

This was the little Eden from which he had been put out and which he remembered. Children appear to forget their griefs easily but they never get over them. Richard had never got over his. Separated from his parents, he used to pray for them every night. "God bless Mummy, God bless Daddy, God bless everybody, and keep us all safe for the night, Amen." Then he heard of their deaths.

So he learned that prayers did not work. Yet he was still a Christian. Christ had cried out, "Oh, my God, why hast Thou forsaken me?"

Those old Victorians, even immensely clever ones, had been able to believe that they would all meet again and be happy in Heaven. He envied them. It was obviously ridiculous. What would he be if he met his mother and father again? An old man? Lucky Victorians. Oh, to go back in time to lovely childhood and be with his dear mother and father again!

Lucky Victorians. Lucky dead, beneath their lichenous stones. Lucky Borrett, pooh-poohing the future. Time for lunch. He started on his way.

Eleven

"It looks as if the weather is going to turn against us after all." Mr Menant stood at the window looking out, hands slipped flat into his jacket pockets with thumbs protruding. Most of his guests were seated at the luncheon table.

Moving from inland before the wind, floes of white cloud were gathering in the sky like jigsaw pieces tentatively laid out, steadily narrowing the runnels of pale blue between them. Below them the force of the wind showed in transparent puffs and scarves of mist streaming fast over the Downs. To the south there was no expanse of blue sky into which one might hope for the cloud to pass leaving clear sky behind. In that direction the cloud roof was unbroken and slaty with rain. As the clouds moved, shadow moved across the landscape and all the brightness went out of its colours.

"As a landowner you should be pleased," Mr Argent said.

"I speak as your host."

"I should find a little rain invigorating," Miss Snell said.

F.J. had been scratching at the table-cloth with a fork as if sketching some diagram to serve a private train of thought. He looked up. "Are we really reduced to talking about the weather?"

Miss Snell said, "Your cricket is at stake."

"Tomorrow is another day."

"Then propose a more rewarding theme, Mr Dobbs, and we shall all be in your debt."

"Improving conversation was the last thing I had in mind. People hound me with it."

"I grieve for you," Miss Snell said. "You give the impression that fame is hardly worth having."

"Sometimes I think so." The growl in F.J.'s voice and the abruptness with which he returned to his scratching or sketching were a warning of dismissal to them all. Miss Snell turned away from him and with undisturbed serenity engaged Mr Argent in talk.

F.J. was not a surly man but to be rude was a privilege of fame which it sometimes relieved his feelings to exercise. His ill-humour had been gathering all day, like the clouds.

First there had been Redington, on the morning walk. Not content with getting F.J.'s promise to attend the conference on sweated labour, he had gone on to suggest what F.J. should say at that assembly. He was a man impervious to hints. F.J. had tried, pleasantly enough at first, to head him off, but he had persisted in the most irritating way, going doggedly on from one proposed subject heading to the next, until at last, "—and as to the problem of inspection, if you were to touch upon—"

F.J. stopped on the hillside, snapped, "Will you please leave the matter of my speech to me, Redington?" and strode off on his own.

There had also been some by-play with Portia, which the observant Miss Snell had not failed to notice. She knew a good deal about F.J. on the one hand and about young women on the other, and she drew her conclusions.

It had been a matter of small attempted intimacies on the part of the girl. At one moment, when they were strung along a hill-top enjoying a view, Portia went to stand next to F.J. and rested the fingertips of her left hand lightly on his sleeve. He did not move away. He looked round him at the landscape, with a faint smile that included no awareness of her. At last he looked directly at her. He let his gaze linger upon her for a couple of seconds, smiling, melancholy and unyielding. Then he moved away, no more detained by her fingertips than he might have been by a strand of cobweb.

Later, when he was walking alone in front of them, Portia hastened to catch up with him and said, "F.J., do you *really* think art is not important?"

"No, I don't think that."

"What *do* you think, then?"

"I've written it all down, you know."

"Well, I think——" and she embarked upon a discourse of which gusts of wind carried back to Miss Snell only the earnest cadences. F.J. strode at her side, letting his empty, smiling eyes rove over the landscape, and answering with an occasional patient, "Yes," or the "Yes, yes," with which one might humour a child.

Portia talked on, undeterred, her voice betraying that drive of eagerness to impress him which he had heard so often. They came to the edge of a rutted chalk track. He stopped. The smile with which he confronted her was more sad and gentle than ever. He said, "My dear, sweet girl, you mustn't think me churlish, but there are times when a writer is claimed by thoughts with which he has to be alone. It's most inconvenient."

Her direct look answered his for a second. Then she said, stolidly, like a hockey-playing schoolgirl, "Sorry."

She rejoined the others and was, Miss Snell thought, a little too animated.

Now she came into the room for luncheon. She had established a kind of punctuality of lateness. For luncheon one expected her just after the first course had been served, and here she was, on time. "Might we not," Mr Argent was saying, "improve the shining hour—? Ah, Miss Menant!"

The men bobbed up and down as she dropped into her chair across the table from Richard. She said, "Do go on, Mr Argent. How are we to improve the shining hour?"

"I was about to suggest that, since it looks somewhat chilly out, we might improve our acquaintance with your beautiful house."

"Oh, yes," Mrs Redington said, "let us have a tour."

"My father is only waiting to be asked," Portia said.

Mr Menant laughed. "I should enjoy it."

"He is an excellent guide. But you must remember to give him sixpence at the end of it. It's the tips as keeps us going."

From the end of the table, Mrs Menant, "Your sense of humour, my dear, can be a little trying."

Richard was far away in his own thoughts when Portia's voice reached the core of his mind.

"Am I?"

He saw her smiling across the table at him. The smile was unqualified, charming. His eyes engaged with hers, she said, "Am I trying, Richard?"

It was confusion again for him. He said, "Not to me."

"Am I trying to you, Mr Dobbs?"

F.J. was now vigorously cutting up beef. He cast up a smiling glance at her, shook his head and returned to his task.

142

"Ah," Portia said. "Mr Dobbs is still busy with his thoughts. He was busy with his thoughts all this morning. That is because he is a famous writer."

"Portia!" Mrs Menant sat upright and outraged. "I will not have you talking to Mr Dobbs like that."

"But Mr Dobbs and I are friends. Are we not, Mr Dobbs?"

F.J. raised his smile to her again, nodded, and bent once more to the mastication of his meat.

"You are the only one who is nice to me, Richard." As long as Richard had known Portia, there had always been a barb or a bait in her voice. She was talking in her new voice now, milky and innocent, with neither barb nor bait. "I wish you had come with us this morning."

And in spite of the tumult of thought in which he was struggling, something melted in his breast. "I'm sorry I couldn't."

"I bet it was dreadfully boring in church."

"Do you ever go?"

Mr Menant said, "Sometimes Portia is good enough to keep me company."

Portia spoke again in her schoolgirl voice. "The vicar writes awful essays for some old church journal. When they're rejected he reads them as sermons."

Richard emitted the sound he thought was called for : a brief, idiot laugh, although his whole being was taken up with immense, incredible questions. He said, "It sounded like it."

He only wanted to be left alone but Portia's eyes were on him, frank and clear as they never had been before, as she said in her new voice, "I don't think it'll rain. Let's go out this afternoon."

He thought his heart had stopped for a second. Then

he said, "I think I should like to see over the house," and looked down at his plate.

She smiled and said, "Oh," her mouth shaping the word roundly.

In desperation, in his inability at all to understand, he fell back upon his thoughts and upon the question he had not so far dared to voice aloud. "F.J. – do you ever read the Bible?"

"Yes. Do you?"

"I am thinking of the story of Joseph in the Old Testament. His dreams, you know. The prophetic dreams by which he established his influence over Pharaoh. The fat kine and the lean kine. All that."

"Legends of a primitive tribe. A tribe that has always invented myths to exaggerate its own importance. What is the drift of your questioning?"

"Have you no scientific interest in such myths?"

"No more than in any other fairy tales."

Miss Snell, between Richard and F.J., said, "You make a sad admission, Mr Dobbs, if you have no regard to the importance of fairy tales."

"Matter of opinion."

"And it is hardly scientific of you to dismiss legends and myths, of whatever tribe, as unimportant. Now will you tell me, Mr Latt, what you are getting at?"

"I think myths are important, too," Richard said. "I am not suggesting that we debate the literal truth of the Old Testament. I think we all understand the nature of such a collection of documents. But I want to know about its significance. Here is an ancient, and I think profound legend, about dreams of precise prophetic significance."

"And," Miss Snell said, "as the anthropologists tell us, with counterparts in popular legend in all sorts of unlikely places, from Iceland to Australasia. Why are these legends so universal? Because they are true."

F.J. uttered a loud, derisive, "Ha!"

"Not literally true. I suppose this particular legend was transmitted by bards and story-tellers from one generation to the next, and sprang from the doings of a Canaanite adventurer at the Egyptian court."

"A typical wheedling Court Jew," F.J. said, "his wiles given a holy gloss by his resourceful descendants."

"That was only the beginning," said Miss Snell. "Why did the myth last? A myth endures when it symbolises some constant factor in human belief – that is to say, experience."

Richard gazed at her as if she were his saviour. "Experience?"

"Yes. Myth in human life is a treasury far richer than our wretched accumulation of written knowledge. It preserves and passes on perceptions that have reverberated in the human mind from the earliest stages of man's fully human existence. It is the literature of the unconscious mind."

"The unconscious mind." F.J. put down his knife and fork. "I thought we would come to that."

"Surely – " intoned Mr Argent, "the Scriptures—"

"Forgive us, Mr Argent." Miss Snell spoke magisterially. "Mr Dobbs and I have moved on to other ground. Yes, Mr Dobbs, the unconscious mind."

"Freud!" F.J. uttered the name in a tone of disgust.

"Freud!" This was Mrs Menant, her mimic scorn failing to conceal the fact that she had never heard of the name.

"Freud," Miss Snell repeated calmly.

F.J. said, "For the last twelve months pretentious idiots have been prattling about that man."

"I am rebuked," Miss Snell said.

Redington said, "Isn't that the fellow Havelock Ellis goes on about."

Mrs Menant was on surer ground. "Ah! Mr Ellis! Yes!"

"I had the good fortune," said Miss Snell, "to hear Professor Freud lecture last year at Clark University, when I was in the United States."

"A Hebrew quack, I believe," Redington put in. "Vienna is full of them."

Richard murmured, "*Die Traumdeutung,*" and felt his face burn scarlet under Miss Snell's quick, stern glance.

She uttered a fierce, "Young man—"

He murmured, still sounding as if he were confessing to some crime, "I read it at Göttingen."

"There is more in you than meets the eye," she said briskly and turned once more upon her adversaries. "Let us have done with Court Jews and Hebrew quacks, my friends. Professor Freud talked to us about dreams."

"He will have an immense following among servant girls," said F.J.

She ignored him "—the deeper, unconscious layer of our minds in which the greater part of our experience is stored and ferments is censored by us, but it does not sleep when we sleep. It is set free to create our dreams, which thus have great significance if we learn to interpret them. They give shape to our experience in symbolic form. So do fairy tales. So do legends."

Richard took another plunge. "What about waking visions?"

"At that point I stop," Miss Snell said. "I am not a mystic."

"Thank you," said F.J. "And you will do better not to traipse after this year's crop of charlatans. I speak as a scientist."

"You are not a scientist, Mr Dobbs. You are a wonderful populariser of science."

F.J.'s manner grew stiff. "I have made a few prophecies of my own—"

"You have," Miss Snell said, "and I do not find you more believable than the Scriptures."

Portia, in her encounter with F.J., had become sensitive enough to his moods to see that he was easily wounded and she longed to inflict a wound. She also longed to take an impressive part in this, to her, impressive colloquy. "Are your prophecies accepted by scientists, Mr Dobbs?"

"By many scientists."

"The most eminent belong to the Royal Society, do they not?"

"Oh," he said, "the old men. The congealing minds."

"It is said that you would like to belong to that Society. Surely that must be untrue."

F.J. stood up. "I am going to lie down. You will have to excuse me from your tour."

"The Sussex iron industry dates from the time of the Romans." Mr Menant was delivering his lecture on the main landing. "It was dormant for centuries but was revived in Tudor times. The ironmasters prospered greatly and by the early seventeenth century they had built many of the finest houses in the region. One of them built Ashtons. His forge was by the river, about six hundred yards downstream from the bridge at the bottom of the garden. All the ironwork in the house, including the fire-backs and the outside gates, goes back to this period. The industry survived until the early seventeenth century, but as the foundations of the industrial revolution were laid in the Midlands and the North – cheap coal instead of char-coal – so the industry down here died out. The iron-masters' houses went down in the world and survived as farmhouses. This was a farmhouse until my predecessor restored it in the eighteen-seventies. I have continued his work."

There was a murmur of approbation from his audience. He said, "We shall go up to the top and come down. There is not a great deal upstairs but the run of the rafters is worth seeing. I could look at English oak beams for ever."

He opened the little door to the upper staircase and the party trooped through; all except Portia and Richard, whom she had gripped by the forearm. She said, "I want to talk to you."

She opened the door of the study. He followed her in. It was a large austere room with walls panelled in oak and bare, polished floorboards. The far end was lined with glass-fronted bookcases. Against the rear wall was a cabinet of sporting guns. Next to it was a big unpolished table on which lay piles of shabby folders full of papers : and at the table a plain wooden armchair. On the other side of the room, beneath a long window with a wide ledge, was a small eighteenth-century parquetry writing desk with much lacquered brass decoration and a gilded beechwood chair with grey tapestry in a floral design. It was plain to see which side of the room Mrs Menant had appropriated. Portia said, "This is the best fireback in the house."

Richard looked into the big fireplace. The iron back depicted in relief the figure of a man in the clothing of the Commonwealth. She said, "This is supposed to be the man who built the house."

"Yes?"

"Richard—" She was silent. Then she spoke as if with effort. "It would be demeaning to talk about what has happened."

"Yes."

"But I had to talk to you."

He waited. She said, "You may not believe me but I cannot bear you to think ill of me."

"I don't."

"There is no need to be kind. I can't explain my feelings to you. You may think I've not behaved very well to you—" She waited for a denial. He waited, too. She went on, "I'm sorry. I'm an impossible person. I can't help being as I am. But I do care most deeply what you think about me. I can't leave you with – a misunderstanding in your mind. I must say something."

He murmured, "Portia, there's no need."

"My lips are sealed. How can I talk to you about – about *that*? But there are things you do not know about. Things that can pass between a – a man of experience and a girl of none. Illusions about a man who is called great. Promises – that count for nothing when it is too late. Undertakings that are broken."

Richard said, "It's too painful for you—"

"I must bear pain, Richard. I've already borne worse. I am afraid of appearing absurd—"

"No."

"You are not a bigot, nor am I, in matters of morality, of behaviour. Neither of us believes that people are –

tied – by old conventions— But it is one thing to be free, and another to be made a fool of—" Her gaze at him was imploring. Tears made her eyes bright.

"Oh, Portia—" Richard's voice became hoarse. "Never—"

She cried, "I can never tell you what that man has done to me."

"Please," he muttered and stepped closer to her.

She managed a wan smile through her tears.

He said, "Nothing has happened, nothing, nothing, nothing—"

"Richard—"

The door opened and Mrs Menant came in. She gave them a sharp, head-turning glance. Her lips were pursed censoriously. In a second she conveyed that in her view her daughter could do better than Richard. "How extraordinary," she said. "I thought you were with Mr Menant."

Portia said, "We came in to look at the fireback."

"Of course. I have come in here to write for a while. Perhaps you would both of you not mind—?"

"No," Portia said. She and Richard went out. She closed the door and said, "Let's go down to the garden."

He followed her down the stairs. Half-way down the first flight he stopped. He saw one of his pictures in front of him.

It was in the air between him and the great staircase window; as if framed by the edges of the window.

It was the picture he called The Moujik. He had seen it twice before. In the foreground was a Russian peasant. Any advanced playgoer of the day or anyone who had read Mrs Garnett's translations of Tolstoy's novels would have recognised him. He wore a long sheepskin coat and a high sheepskin hat. He had a dirty yellow beard and dirty yellow hair stuck out from under his cap. He was the sort of peasant held up by Count Tolstoy as the embodiment of all the elemental wisdom and goodness of the earth. Platon Kharateyev, as it might be.

But this moujik looked neither wise nor good. In his right hand he carried to the top of its swing a great cavalry sabre. On the front of his sheepskin cap was a small red star with five points. Behind him were diagonal rows of trees with branches smothered in blossom of palest pink. There was a tree in front of him.

And – this was what made the picture the most mysterious of all those that Richard had seen – the peasant had evidently just hacked down the tree in the foreground. The trunk in its cloud of blossom had fallen to one side, and spurting straight up from the stump was a fountain of blood.

He stood on the stairs, mesmerised by the picture. Portia had paused and turned round. She said, "Richard, what's the matter?"

He did not move. She raised her voice. "Richard—"

He stood as if he could not hear her. Her voice roughened, "Richard, are you mad? *Say* something!"

He had recognised something in this enigmatic picture that he had not discerned before. He knew what the trees were. He could not steady his breathing. "Portia, I'm sorry—Oh, I'm sorry—"

She cried, "Are *you* trying to make a fool of me?"

She turned and sped downstairs. Richard remained in his trance. He did not know for how long. He heard the sound of voices and footsteps. His senses returned and he went up to the landing. He did not dare to go downstairs after Portia and he could not think where to hide. The door of the West Bedroom opened. F.J. stood in the doorway. "Hallo," he cried. "I heard you out there with milady. Had enough of her? Come in."

Richard went into the bedroom. F.J. closed the door. A moment later they heard Mr Menant and his party emerge on to the landing and go downstairs. "I've been wanting to have a word with you," F.J. said. "You seem to have some ideas churning about in your noddle. Tell me about them."

Twelve

F.J. drew an armchair away from the wall. "Sit down, sit down. Be the guest of honour's guest of honour."

The walls of the guest of honour's bedroom were simply whitewashed, the oak beams dividing them into rectangles. F.J. said, "Menant's the one with the taste. This house is his mistress. His only one, I gather. He lets her buy her fallals but he won't let her put a finger on the house."

"I thought your room would be rather grand and big. Mine is nearly as big as this."

"But I've got a four-poster." F.J. bounced like a child on the edge of the canopied bed. "And Perugino and Burne-Jones on the wall." He put on his music-hall Cockney accent. "Cor blimey, culcher! Now then, Richard Latt—"

It was a physical fact that Richard's head was bursting with his own preoccupations. He felt as if some fierce gas were pressing hard upon the inside of his skull. F.J. said, "What was all this fiddle-faddle at luncheon? About dreams and whatnot?"

"Oh— I was just – speculating."

"Excellent woman, Rosetta—"

"Rosetta?"

"Miss Snell. Still a good looker. Do you know, she has had the most passionate love for a man, married man, since she was young. Reciprocated, too. And they've never laid a finger on each other. I'll swear to that. Rum, eh? People are strange. She does go on, though, doesn't she? Picks up things she doesn't understand. Women do."

"Do they?"

"Oh, yes, take my word. Equality's all right. But they're still built to fulfil the biological division of labour, and the male has the greater brain capacity. Jealous, too. Another feminine characteristic. Did you notice that? She got quite catty when I put her right."

Richard said, rather miserably, "I see."

"You mustn't take notice of all this mystical poppy-cock. Drawing-room pseudo-science. A constant bubble on the surface of polite talk. Like marsh gas. Stick to science, my boy."

Words burst out of Richard. He had reached the point at which it was as impossible for him to hold back an outpouring of his troubles as, otherwise distressed, it would have been impossible not to vomit. "F.J. – do you think I'm mad?"

"Eh?"

"It's what's been happening to me—" And it all came out, in a rush that was only punctuated by Richard's need to take breath.

He said that he had been having pictures, or halluci-nations. He broke off to describe his encounters with the doctors since his accident – concerning which he did not linger to tell the truth. He went on to describe his pictures one by one carefully. He broke off after he had told about Aunt Marian's death. "Shall I stop? Are you fed up with this?"

F.J. sat on the edge of his bed, head down, frowning. "No. No. Go on."

Richard went on to the others. When he had described
The Blacks, F.J. muttered,

> "Whatever happens, we have got
> The Maxim gun and they have not."

"Oh! – I'm sorry?"

"Never mind. Carry on."

Richard told him about The Moujik. "It was different
from most of the others, you see. I mean, it wasn't real,
not like a photograph."

"No."

"But today I saw what it meant. He had cut down a
cherry tree."

"And?"

"It was Madame Ranevsky's."

"*The Cherry Orchard.* You saw it, did you?"

"Oh, yes, Aunt Marian and I go to all the Stage Society
shows."

"Shaw made them put it on. He got me along there.
So you believe in Rosetta's symbols, do you? Never mind,
go on."

There was another unreal picture. Richard called it
The Circus. There was no circus in it. It was an outdoor
scene, and the background consisted of the rooftops and
upper storeys of houses in a poor part of London; West
London, probably, looking towards the Thames, for the
types of houses were easily recognisable and the distance,
as distinguishing landmarks, were Big Ben and the towers
of the Palace of Westminster. But this familiar scene was
broken by many unfamiliar things. To start with, the
landscape was dotted with narrow towers, plain rectangular affairs the nearer of which seemed to be made
mostly of glass, which rose to astonishing heights. There

were dozens of them rising out of the sea of London slates, all the way to the hilly skyline of the Surrey suburbs. Still more astonishing was the main feature in the foreground. It was a wide road with a plain grey surface. It was wider than any road Richard knew, and it had six lanes marked out by white lines, three going one way and three going the other. But the most surprising thing about this road was that it was built on a kind of immense bridge, stretching so far that the end could not be seen, and it was almost at the level of the rooftops. Streets ran below it, with traffic passing underneath the elevated road. This road carried a great deal of traffic—

F.J., who confined his interruptions to occasional brief comments and questions, asked a question now. "But why do you call it The Circus?"

"Because of the faces – I'll come to that. Please let me explain—"

The traffic on the elevated road was heavy, and it consisted of what were recognisably motor-cars. They were odd-looking vehicles, smooth and elongated and totally enclosed, with large windows all round, painted in every possible bright colour and flimsy-looking as if stamped out of thin metal like children's toys. They had small wheels with fat tyres and enclosed hubs and they gleamed with strips of bright silver metal. There was no mistaking what they were, though, with their steering wheels and their drivers and passengers. There were also lorries, not greatly different from present-day lorries, except that they were not so high, their bodies were as often as not apparently made of metal and some of them were of immense length. And all this traffic was halted; because right in front of the picture there had been a fearful accident.

"I'm coming to the faces," he said. "Please be patient."
A motor-car right at the front of the picture had swerved
broadside on, and six others behind had one by one
crashed each into the one in front of it, some carried by
their speed on top of other vehicles in a sprawling pile
of crumpled metal. The nearer door of the front vehicle
had flown open and the driver, his lower body crushed,
had fallen across the seat, his head out of the car, his
blood pouring down from the deeply-cushioned seat on
to the roadway and purling in a widening delta of
streams towards the viewer.

"And you see," Richard said, "you see, all the vehicles
had stopped but nobody was doing anything to help. I'll
tell you what I mean about the faces. All the people in all
the other motors were gaping out of their windows and
grinning and talking as if they were at a show. One man
stood on the bonnet of his motor with what looked like
a small camera. I think he was taking pictures. And you
know those houses, all those rows of slummy red brick
houses with their top windows looking on to the road –
well, all those windows were crammed with people, and
they were all laughing, and pointing, and eating, and
holding up children to see. All I could see in the picture
was hundreds and hundreds of stupid white blobs of
faces with the little dabs and blobs for eyes and noses
and mouths all grinning as if they were at a show. And
I know it's silly, but it was what haunted me most about
this picture, and I called it The Circus because all those
people reminded me of what I'd read about the old
Roman circuses."

F.J. nodded. "And it was London."

"Yes. You couldn't mistake it."

Richard waited for a verdict. F.J. said, "When we

look at your hallucinations – I'm going to use your own word – they consist of two sorts. These strange pictures which I am going to call long-range, and two which we shall call short-range."

"Two of them have come true. Precisely and unmistakably. I do beg you to believe me about that."

F.J. said, "Mm."

Even a few moments of silence were torment to Richard. "Please tell me. *Am* I mad? Should I see an alienist?"

"Who was the brain man you saw?"

Richard named the specialist. F.J. said, "I know him. Best man in the country. Meet him at the Athenaeum. If he said there's nothing wrong, there's nothing wrong. Your memory is certainly all right."

"Then what does it all mean? What shall I do?"

"Steady on. All the pictures, long-range and short, have one common factor."

"Yes—" Richard spoke with a betraying promptness. "Blood."

"Assuredly there is nothing wrong with your mind, my lad. In every picture there is a pool or stream of blood."

"I suppose an alienist would call that a monomania."

"Not so fast. Let's follow our clue. Blood. That is the link between your two kinds of vision."

"Vision?"

"For the moment I use words for simple convenience. Without prejudice. I think your two short-term visions – those that have come true – were sports, freaks. They should not have happened but there was blood in each of them. So they found their way into your mental circuit as it were. Only because of the blood. And served as warnings to you, as clues to the nature of the others."

"You are saying that the others are true."

"I am building up a hypothesis."

"But you do take it seriously?"

"Be quiet." F.J. pondered for a little while, then he threw his head up, radiant with his broad, genial smile. "By Jove, what a fine story!"

Richard felt a sinking in his breast. "But what about me?"

"What a tale it would make! Just suppose a man, by some freak – perhaps through a knock on the head – what do we know as yet about the human brain? – finds himself endowed with some perception – just flashes of perception which he cannot even interpret – of the human future. Just suppose! By thunder, I have already treated of time as a dimension—"

"I know. But please—"

"And what a fulfilment of my prophecies!" F.J. stood up and began to walk about, excited. His colloquy now was with himself. "That shattered room and the dead woman. What is it but a scene of war, of London destroyed in a future war? You know my story about the ultimate war – the atom split and used as a terrible weapon. That's it, that's it. And your elevated roadway – you remember my city of the future?"

"Yes," Richard sat inert and did not try to say any more.

F.J.'s step was light with joy. "Suppose we took you seriously? What a vindication of me! Oho!—" He clapped his hands and rubbed them together. "It would be one in the eye for those old fools at the Royal. Who, I shall ask them, is the scientist now? Eh? Who?"

Richard said, "But no-one must know about this."

"Eh?"

"It was in confidence. Please."

"But this is a story for— My goodness, I can—"

"F.J., please, please, you mustn't tell anyone."

F.J. paused and looked down at him. Then, "All right. All right, young Richard. It shall be as you say. Between the two of us."

"Thank you." Richard stood up. "But now, what can I do?"

"I shall think upon it," F.J. said. "We'll talk more."

Voices in the garden were receding. F.J. went to look out of the window. "They have gone to the woods. I shall have another nap and see what inspiration it brings. Off you go, Richard Latt."

Thirteen

F.J. spoke no more in private to Richard that day. When they met he favoured Richard with a smile. Once, for a moment, he dropped a hand on Richard's shoulder; as if to say, "bear up", or to suggest that they were the sharers of a secret.

Richard was greatly relieved by his confession. There was no rain in the afternoon and the darker clouds did not move in from the sea; but a combination of high summer heat and a roof of cloud made the air somewhat close. Richard's spirits had recovered sufficiently for him to join in the remaining diversions of the day. He took part in a game of croquet. Portia also played. She was as cool as if nothing had happened between them. Her glance crossed his unconcernedly. She did not speak to him except, indifferently, concerning the game.

Before dinner Portia appeared in yet a further dress and produced a further effect. She was all in white silk, and this time she had allowed herself an ornament, a long gold chain, very fine, with no pendant. It set off her fair hair and slender figure remarkably enough for Mr Argent to chant, "Clothed in white samite, mystic, wonderful."

F.J. said, "I bet nobody knows what samite is."

Miss Snell spoke kindly, as to a pupil. "A rich silken fabric worn in the Middle Ages, sometimes interwoven with gold."

"I wish I could get some," Portia said. "I love dress-making."

F.J. looked at her and said, "Good Lord!"

"Oh, yes." She threw him a sidelong, saucy glance. "Do you think I spend pots of father's money? I make all my own dresses. This one only cost me twenty-one bob."

"Portia," her mother said, "I should prefer you to talk English," and she flipped a finger to Hawker who stood in the doorway and who intoned in response, "Dinner is served, madam."

During the meal Portia, again displaying a new self, held forth a great deal, turning from one neighbour to another or addressing the table in general, with much rapid speech, an unwonted freedom of gesture and an air of imperious animation. Her voice was pitched a little higher than usual and to Richard her gaiety seemed nervous and brittle. She showed no awareness of Richard except as a face in the audience.

After dinner Richard contrived to walk alone in the garden, on the excuse of a headache. The clouds were moving away. They were like a roof being slid open, revealing more and more of the sky as infinity, deepest blue enriched by darkness and pricked by innumerable brilliant stars. Occasionally a rise and fall of breeze brought a sigh from the wood. The air in the garden was scented.

The windows of the drawing-room were open. Richard walked to and fro, and from a decent distance glanced in at the house party each time he passed. Portia was curled up in one corner chair, the Siamese cat in the opposite corner. Mr Argent leaned back in his chair, listening prayerfully. Mrs Menant sat upright and kept her guests under prim and censorious survey, fingertips hooked together in front of her. F.J. stood astride in front of the fireplace and Mr Menant, his interlocutor, lounged, easy and genial, at one end of the Knole settee. Framed in the windows, lit in bright yellow, it looked like a stage scene carefully composed by a producer. The conversation came clearly to Richard.

"If you are going to work Africans," F.J. was saying, "you might as well work them to the limit. They do not wish to work, not as we require them to, and it is humbug for these scandalmongers to suggest that two strokes of the lash are more reprehensible than one."

"What the Belgians did under Leopold," Mr Menant said, "was considerably worse than that."

"I dare say they are still doing it, though more discreetly," F.J. said. "I should take Albert's reforms with a pinch of salt."

"And you defend the extortion of wealth from a helpless population by terror and mass murder?"

"The Belgians make a profit. That is what colonies are for. It is a matter of efficiency."

Mr Menant said, "Cruelty is not efficient. It is exceedingly wasteful."

"But you trade with them," Redington said.

"I have no trade with the Congo. I have no need to."

"Ah," Redington said. "Is that morality? You are a good businessman and you do well enough elsewhere. But if you needed to – and after all, it is a question of keeping up this beautiful house, of putting money into this estate so beloved to you, of giving your talented wife the setting she needs and of providing suitably for your daughters – if you needed to, you would have to, and then you would find some moral justification."

163

"I should like to think not."

Miss Snell said, "You were, if I may make the reference without discourtesy, a supporter of the South African War."

Mr Menant permitted himself a comfortable stretch of the backbone. "That's going back a bit."

"It was," Mrs Redington said, "a touchstone."

"Of what?"

"Of genuine belief in human rights."

"My dear friends," Mr Argent said, "here we are, the recipients of Mr Menant's magnificent hospitality, and we are pressing him upon most personal matters. I am moved to cry, 'Enough'."

"Oh, no," Mr Menant said. "Nothing personal. Or rather, how can one talk about any important matter of politics without being personal? Since we are all, in our various ways, politicians. Of course I supported the South African War. It is true that I conduct most of my trade with South Africa and that it has multiplied since that war. But I insist that my support was one of principle and was not based on self-interest."

"Hear, hear," F.J. said. "I am sick of all you tender hearts who deplore the Imperial system and live well upon its fruits. And I am doubly sick of that beastly little demagogue Lloyd George who opposed the war for the notoriety he could get out of it."

"I wonder," Miss Snell said. "A human being is a tissue of contradictions. The most deplorable person may sometimes be moved by principles to act bravely and to his own disadvantage."

"No action of Lloyd George's ever has been or ever will be to his disadvantage," F.J. said. "I support you, Menant. The Imperial system means efficiency, whether or not this or that corner is worked wastefully as you allege to be the case with the Congo. It means a central-ised use of the resources of the earth to the ultimate good of all. It is no shame to you that your trade with South Africa has prospered since that part of the world came under the flag. It simply shows that the area itself has prospered now that it enjoys the resources and governing talents of a Great Power—"

"The greatest Power – " Mr Argent put in.

" – and that you have, in consequence, benefited, as has everyone else. Perhaps even as a businessman you have contributed to that betterment by fostering trade intelligently."

"I hope so," Mr Menant said.

"And as for human rights, my dear Jane," F.J. said to Mrs Redington, "what worse enemies of the African and his rights, such as they are, could there be than those wretched bigoted Boers with their rhinoceros-hide whips? Your native is always better off under the protection of the Great Power."

"Ah," Mr Menant said. "Only if the Power is wise and humane as we are. Brutes like the Germans and Belgians are not fit to have colonies."

Richard turned away and paced the garden path. At the end he came near to the gate beyond which lay the servants' yard, the outbuildings of their quarters on three sides and the kitchen at the back of the house. The kitchen, too, was brightly lit. Loud talk and laughter came to him. He could see Hawker pouring beer from a bottle. Here, too, was a house-party of sorts. He continued his walk. He did not go into the wood. It was ghostly among the trees and the scurry of even small animals, plainly heard, touched town-bred Richard with a child's fright.

Some time had passed when he arrived back at the house. In the drawing-room goodnights were being said. People went out of the room. Portia had already gone. Only the Redingtons remained.

"I shall read for a while," Mrs Redington said. "You may go up if you are tired."

"Wherever F.J. is," her husband said, "he imagines he is delivering a lecture. I wonder how that woman got him."

"Where there are daughters, F.J. goes."

"And wives."

Mrs Redington turned an open gaze up to her husband. "Oh, no, you do not know the man. His addiction nowadays is to *fruit vert*. Or at least fruit ungathered."

"You know him, it appears," her husband said, and settled down in his chair with an *Illustrated London News*.

"Thank you," Mrs Redington said with a touch of tartness, "for keeping me company."

Richard felt that he had spied enough and moved away. Round the corner of the house came Portia, in a drift of white draperies. He stood still. She came to him and at once slipped her hands in his arm, to join them. She said, "Richard, will you come to my room?"

He looked at her pale, strained face. It seemed forever before he could speak. "My dear girl, it's not possible."

She kept her earnest, seeking scrutiny upon him. "Now I am damned by you. The slut."

"No. It is I who always let the right moment go by. And curse myself when it is too late."

She said, "Yes."

"Forgive me."

She wafted away.

Fourteen

F.J. came out of the study a contented man, his host at his shoulder. The distant thump of mallets told of preparations for the cricket game. The weather was cool but bright, just, as F.J. remarked to Mr Menant, the ticket. The conference about F.J.'s investment portfolio had been productive. Not only had he received sound advice about his shares in general, but Mr Menant had promised him a slice of a new issue of gold stocks which would be subscribed before the public ever got its nose in. All, almost, was well for F.J. on this August Monday morning.

Almost. As they went downstairs he said, "I do not wish to usurp your captaincy of the house team—"

"My dear fellow," Mr Menant said, "I would be delighted to have you captain the team but, you see, it is expected of me. It is a sort of feudal matter. I am afraid my work-people would regard it as a sort of abdication."

"I would not usurp your seignorial rights for worlds. But I have a certain experience of cricket—"

"I know, I know, dear F.J. If you were not famous as a writer I am sure you would be famous as a cricketer."

"I have a certain feel for the game. But above all—" They had reached the ground floor— "I know how to win games."

"Oh—" Mr Menant threw back his head and let his

easy-going laugh resound in the hall for a few moments. "Winning. That is the least of my concerns."

"What is the use of playing games if you are not out to win?" A slight testiness crept into F.J.'s voice. "This damned good-loser stuff. Dilettantism. It's a threat to the Empire, you take my word. And arrogant at that. Condescending to your inferiors."

"Let us try to win by all means. I merely confess that to me the game is the thing."

"It is all a matter of tactics. Co-ordination. Preparation. Games interest me because they are a form of warfare—"

"Ah," Mr Menant said. "We all know of your profound interest in and talent for warfare. Perhaps if you were neither a famous writer nor a famous cricketer, you would be a famous general."

Much was known and talked in their set about the war room at F.J.'s house, in which hundreds of toy soldiers were marshalled with artillery, camps, forts, wagons and all the other necessary paraphernalia. F.J. spent hours at a time in this room with his children and sometimes with favoured guests.

"I am merely suggesting that we assemble the house team in good time – that is to say, before midday – so that I can try them out, decide on proper dispositions for them and instruct them thoroughly."

"Dear chap, I wish we could. But apart from ourselves and young Latt, the house team consists of my one non-aged gardener and his boy, both of whom are busy at the cricket field – and I dare not disturb them if all is to be ready in time – of two keepers, whose cottages are far apart in the woods, Borrett, who has driven into Lewes to bring Captain Smethwick, our umpire, and three men from the home farm whose dwellings are also scattered. How could I round them up before lunch?"

"Atrocious planning."

"Indeed. I plead guilty, F.J. But after luncheon, as soon as they are all here, I shall marshal them and you shall instruct them." Mr Menant's smile was as open as if he were not aware of F.J.'s frown. "And now you must forgive me. There is so much to do. I must go to the field. Mrs Menant has all the village to feed this afternoon and is no doubt in the kitchen counting the jam tarts. The children do love it. I must for a while leave my guests to their own devices."

Off he went. F.J. hung about in the hall, looking with distaste at faded tapestries. His good humour had cooled away. He was more than a little nettled. Merely because of that talk about shares, Menant appeared to imagine that their relationship had changed. He no longer showed that deference to the guest of honour to which F.J. was so sensitive. On the contrary, F.J., a thin-skinned man in the company of those born to ways he had only in recent years made his own, felt that Menant had become condescending, as if he had dispensed some largesse to his guest. F.J. had not been unaware of those little conversational ironies.

He went into the drawing-room. Its only occupant was Portia, reading. She put down her book and said, "Good morning."

"Good morning." He sat down next to her. He picked up the book. "Henry James. My dear girl, how *can* you?"

"There is no disputing of tastes."

"Those immense, involved unravellings of the trivial."

"The emotions are trivial to some and not to others."

"They are not trivial to me."

"I am glad."

"Our private lives and feelings are so enmeshed with the great public concerns that literature which ignores this fact is trivial."

"Mr James does not ignore the fact. He writes for those who are equipped to understand him."

"Who have you been listening to upon the subject?"

"You judge that I have no mind of my own."

"Dear Portia, this is going all wrong. I judge nothing of the sort. Do let us be friends."

She said, easily, "By all means."

"I hope so. I think a great deal of you."

She smiled. "Thank you, kind sir."

"Put away the rapier, my lamb. I shall not draw. Tell me what you mean to do in London. Shall you work for a degree under the guidance of our admirable Miss Snell?"

"Perhaps. Does the matter interest you?"

"Of course," he said with grave kindness. "Whatever befalls you will always be of interest to me."

"Of remote interest, since we shall not meet."

"Oh, to be sure, we shall meet. There are all sorts of occasions and places. We shall meet as friends meet."

"At your lectures, no doubt. Will you expect to see me among the earnest young ladies who throng to the platform in the hope of a word from you?"

"My dear—" He dropped a hand on hers. "My life is not my own. That's the truth of it. I only ask you to understand. And to let me feel, as this weekend draws to a close, that you are my friend."

She stood up. "I shall," she said, "always, as you ask. In fact, if there be founded a society known as The

Friends of F. J. Dobbs, I shall join it. Excuse me. My mother will be needing help."

She went out of the room.

The cricket field was by the lane, just outside the east wall of the gardens. A small wooden pavilion with a gallery outside had been recently painted. It was the scene of much activity. Two gardeners had brought a handcart piled with cricket gear. Directed by Mr Menant, who stood on the gallery, they began to take armfuls of the gear in to the changing-room, at one end of the pavilion.

A small marquee had risen on the opposite side of the field. Here the villagers would receive their refreshment. Three men moved around it, testing the guylines and giving final taps of the mallet to tent pegs. One of them was Richard, who had, for the sake of occupation, volunteered to help.

A posse of women had already taken possession of the marquee's interior. They were setting up trestle tables, shaking out long tablecloths and starting to unload baskets of plates, utensils and appropriate food. Mrs Menant was in charge of them. Portia, to escape from the house, had accompanied her.

Voices drifted across the field. Through the gate from the lane trooped all the remaining guests, Miss Snell, the Argents, the Redingtons and, in their midst, F.J., who appeared to be discoursing to them like the cicerone of a Cook's Tour.

The group straggled towards the pavilion. Mr Menant waved to them, said a few words to his men and went to meet them. Richard was stooped over a tent peg when he turned his head at the sound of F.J.'s squeaky voice.

He straightened up. He was hot and stiff. He dropped his mallet and hastened to join the newcomers.

"I do hope we are not untimely," Miss Snell said as Mr Menant came up to them. "We must not be a hindrance."

"Not at all," said the host.

"You must blame F.J. if we are," Mr Redington said. "He rounded us up and insisted that we come and help."

"I fear I do not know the man," Mr Argent put in, "who can say Mr Dobbs nay."

"A few willing hands," F.J. said. "Perhaps we can put out chairs or something."

"I shall not hear of it." Their voices had brought Mrs Menant to the door of the marquee and now she joined them, with Portia in attendance. "There are workpeople here for that sort of thing. Blake—" She was calling to one of the gardeners in the pavilion. "Will you bring chairs, at once?"

She had dressed as if to enhance her appearance of command in a somewhat Ruritanian costume of light grey mohair with big cloth buttons and narrow collar both striped in red, with braided military cuffs and big, braided patch pockets fastened by braid tassels.

F.J. said, "We shouldn't have grudged a little hard labour."

Mr Argent reminded them that according to Count Tolstoy labour in the fields was the path to salvation.

"I do assure you," Mr Menant said. Chairs were being rapidly brought. "All's finished. All is in hand. I should like a rest myself. Do, please, be seated."

"I have sent a boy to the house for lemonade," Mrs Menant said.

They settled in the deckchairs, in a rough circle. "Village cricket can be fun," F.J. said, "but it is all slog and no science—"

"When you meet our village team," Mr Menant said, "you will know what the word slog means. Their captain is the blacksmith. We are a democratic village."

"All the same," F.J. said, "for real cricket you must see two good county sides. I went up to Bradford in June to see Yorkshire beat Lancashire by five wickets. That was a game. Rhodes asked me up there. He wasn't too proud to take my advice and he scored ninety-two in the first innings." He went on for some time, talking of his friends in the higher reaches of cricket.

Mr and Mrs Menant listened with befitting expressions of polite interest but from the rest of the group came more and more signs of inattention, re-arrangements of limbs, stares into the far distance. Mr Argent sighed, as he had several times this morning, and remarked once more, "I wonder what is happening at the House."

"Oh, damn the House," F.J. cried. "Today's debate is just a lot of jabber. Snowden assures me the Bill will go through. Now, you think of Hobbs as a batsman, don't you? But I was the one who pointed out to him that there wasn't a finer fieldsman in England at cover point, and you see where he's been placed ever since—"

It was the last day of what to the rest of the party had come in retrospect to seem a longish weekend in the company of the great man. Redington stood up. "I think we've had enough cricket." He turned to Mr Menant. "I see you're putting in trees. Does it repay the effort now that imported wood is so cheap?"

"I do it because I love to see woodlands well kept up," Mr Menant said. "But as to making it pay, I must put modesty aside and remind you that so far I have made everything pay."

F.J. sat in sulky gloom which intensified when he caught a twinkle of mockery in Portia's eyes. It was deuced rude of Redington to interrupt, and typical of these wretched people to talk about timber when he, F.J., was in their midst. "I say—" His interruption sounded like a proclamatory note upon a reed pipe. "I'd like to see that old water-mill you get your electric power from, Menant. Let's go down there."

"We went yesterday," said Redington.

"But don't let us keep you from going." Jane Redington, smiling at him with the malice of an old flame, added to his discomfiture. He stood up. It was an imperative with him to be the centre of things. "Never mind that. Listen, everybody, I'm going to tell you a story."

Hero-worship revived in Mrs Menant's cry, "Oh, that will be an honour."

From Mr Menant, "Is it one you plan to publish?"

"You must advise me about that."

"We?" said Miss Snell.

"Yes. All of you." F.J. surveyed them all. All were attentive. He was satisfied and smiled benignly. "It is an idea. You will tell me what you think of it. Call it a scientific speculation. A poser. As *Tit-Bits* would call it, a teaser."

"We are all ears," Mr Argent said.

"You are familiar with my fictional speculations upon time as a dimension." There were noises of assent. "Suppose, then, that instead of a man travelling through time we have a man who, simply, has flashes of prevision concerning the future."

"Fascinating," Mrs Menant said. At her gesture, a silent maid stole from chair to chair with the lemonade tray.

"He is an ordinary fellow——" He paused and smiled, gently, under his heavy lids at Richard, who presented a stunned face to him. "He has had, let us, oh, let us sketch it in for the sake of the tale, a knock on the head with no ill-effects that the finest of doctors can discern, but perhaps with unknown effects upon the as yet mysterious structure of the human brain – our young man's brain. With the result that from time to time he picks up, if I may use the analogy of the radio wave, a signal from the future. Well?"

There was an interval of general consideration. Then, "I can say nothing about the scientific hypothesis that you propound," Miss Snell said, "but my interest in your tale will lie in what your young man picks up."

"Precisely. He sees pictures. Large coloured photographs of scenes from the future superimposed, as it were, upon the air before him——"

Redington : "How does he know that these pictures are scenes from the future?"

"Because, by some fluke, two of them concern incidents in the very near future, and when these incidents occur he sees the pictures verified down to the last detail."

"And what does he see?" insisted Miss Snell.

"Barbarism." F.J. let this sink in. "I shall not describe the pictures. I must, after all, keep some secrets for the printed page. But he is confronted by a series of scenes which he cannot at first interpret, but which more and more impress themselves upon him as glimpses of a future of barbarism triumphant, of inferior races aswarm like the Goths and the Vandals against the ramparts of

175

Europe, armed to the teeth with the most modern weapons, while the peoples of old Europe are degenerate, sunk in stupidity and greed for sensation, their cities shattered by internecine wars – utterly corrupt, utterly vulnerable."

"You do like to make people's flesh creep," Redington said. "We've had all that in your science tales."

"Precisely," F.J. said. "The young man's visions bear out all that my tales have prophesied."

"Not to be wondered at," Redington said, "since they all spring from your own fertile imagination."

"Ah," F.J. said. "I see I will have to let you into the real secret." Richard sat like stone in his chair. "The idea is not mine. It belongs to our young friend here." He smiled at their chatter of surprise. "Forgive me, young Richard Latt, for betraying your secret, but it is all in fun and among friends. Richard aspires to become a practitioner of my craft. He has confided this story to me. Many minds are better than one, and I am sure that he would like to hear your opinions as well as mine."

"In that case," Miss Snell said, "I do not like to discourage, but frankness serves best. What he adumbrates is impossible."

"Impossible," Mr Argent echoed.

"You know, young man," Redington said, "if you intend to turn a penny by purveying the horrific, private horrors win hands down, every time. Try vampires, the dead walking the earth, or something like Doctor Jekyll."

F.J.'s face became gleeful, "And now, my friends, your comments have brought us to the nub of young Richard's tale. You see, the man who has these visions is in the midst of a group of people exactly like ourselves. He is driven to tell what he has seen and meets with general scepticism – no, I put it too mildly – ridicule. And he is driven to desperation."

"I do not wonder," said Redington. "What else can he expect from a group of people who are not only in their right minds but more than usually well-informed?"

Richard said nothing. He could not meet anybody's eyes. Mr Menant gave him a sympathetic glance. "Oh, come, you really mustn't set upon Richard like that. You're too discouraging. You write your tale, Richard. No matter what we say. You know, one does not need to be credible to sell a tale. You will find a market, I am sure, if you spin your yarn artfully enough. It is no disgrace to start a writing career in the penny dreadfuls. Successful men have done so."

"Hear, hear," his wife said. "I may be able to introduce you to editors when you have done. But you must write first. It is easy to think of a tale but hard to write it."

"Is that all you have to offer him?" F.J. looked round at them. "My dear—" He spoke to Miss Snell. "Will you not say something more positive?"

"Only what I have already said. Education generates itself. Its advance and expansion cannot now be halted. It guarantees against such nightmares as you have described."

"Yes," F.J. said. "And you, Mr and Mrs Redington, will remind us of remorseless melioration."

At the same moment Redington said, "Quite," and his wife said, "Exactly."

Richard stared at the ground with a wild, inward look. It was not one of his pictures that he saw, but the scene around him, and in his mind it had taken on the same frightening quality as his visions. There they all were, lounging in their chairs, sketching graceful gestures with their hands, chattering in their well-bred accents. They took for granted the maidservant moving humbly around them, the women who came out of the marquee and curtseyed and said "By your leave, ma'am," the workmen in the pavilion who touched their caps. They were as unassailable in their dream as the old Victorian was in his conviction of a happy life to come, united with his lost ones in Heaven.

"Menant?"

"Some businessmen are enlightened but most, I fear, are fools. However, they all know on which side their bread is buttered. War has become an economic nonsense and they will not permit it. Nor will the statesmen."

"But—" The one explosive syllable burst from Richard. His courage failed again but he had to go on. "But, sir, only the other night, you were so pessimistic. About the mob and anarchy and all that."

"I? Pessimistic?" Mr Menant, laughing, looked round him in appeal. "Good Heavens, no! I was merely speculating upon what might happen if more scoundrelly upstarts get into politics and turn our people into a bribed mob. But it shan't happen, dear boy. There are too many educated and responsible men who will not allow it. There will be no anarchy. We have policemen at home and forces abroad to nip it in the bud. Instead we have the means to make everyone prosperous and we shall. But, my dear Richard, I do truly congratulate you upon your imaginative powers. I have advised you to find a vocation and perhaps this is it. I do urge you to press on."

F.J. saw Mr Argent waiting with his mouth open and the light of prophecy upon his face. He hastened to forestall. "Mr Argent, we know of your lifelong and unshake-able belief in progress."

"Indeed—"

But F.J. was ruthless. "Mrs Menant?"

"Art contradicts our young friend. Culture contradicts him. I know from my public work that more and more workmen are being taught to behave seriously and re-sponsibly. Women, the mothers of the race, will win their place in the sun and make bloodshed, the sacrifice of their children, impossible. Where is your degeneracy?"

"Portia?"

Portia had all this time lain back in her chair, hands limp at her sides, looking at F.J. and looking at Richard. She remained silent.

"You see, young Richard," F.J. said. "As a writer I say: Ignore the audience at your peril. I, the iconoclast, say so. Be warned, young man."

"But you—" The cry broke from Richard. "Why don't *you* tell them?"

"Tell them what?"

"What *you* think?"

"I?" F.J. was bland and smiling. "What I think is well known. You have read all my books, you have attended my lectures, studied my articles. You know well that I am an optimist—"

"Your stories—"

"Warnings, young man, of what could happen if the human intelligence were not applied. But it will be applied."

There were cries of accord. F.J. had his audience. He was happy. "You know that I have written – I have talked to you this very weekend – of the castes which are being brought inevitably to birth by modern technology."

"The scientists and the airmen," Mrs Menant chanted dutifully.

"And do not forget the mechanics, the intelligent fellows who make the machines and maintain them. Do you think that such castes will let folly triumph? Do you think they will fail to perceive what power is in their hands and to use it beneficently? Dear boy, I am the great optimist. I see a land – if I may borrow from Mr Argent's terminology – of milk and honey."

Richard looked at the ground and said, almost inaudibly, "Blood."

Mr Argent saw his opening. "For we shall build Jerusalem in England's green and pleasant land."

His eyes still downcast, Richard muttered, "Just blood."

"Dear boy," F. J. said, "learn from your reception today. Do not press on along that path. It will lead you down to Gehenna. Visions can be dismissed, like Prospero's cloud-capped towers and gorgeous palaces. Live for today. There is cricket to play."

Richard rose. He kept his head turned away from the gaze of the others, for he was close to tears. "Excuse me. Some work to do."

He went back to the marquee, picked up his mallet and did things with tent pegs.

"Richard—" Portia was at his side. He continued to tap a mallet needlessly. "Why are you so upset?"

He did not answer. She said, "Is it a story?"

His throat was dry. He did not look up at her. "No."

"It's you."

"Yes."

She said quietly, in a faintly wondering tone, "Do you think you're mad?"

"I might be."

She went away.

Kneeling over his tent peg he heard voices recede as the house party trailed away toward the lane gate. They passed along the lane in the direction of the house. When he could hear them no more he stood up and returned to the house by a back path.

A small gate admitted him to one of the gardens, in which was a pergola. Thickly clustered upon this were climbing roses mingled with royal purple blossoms of Jackman's clematis. In this airy tunnel of leaf and blossom he wandered up and down.

He was in a state in which he hardly thought. His mind and body both ached with the shock of F.J.'s betrayal. In time the ache lessened but in its place there returned his old conviction that he was doomed always to be alone. This conviction had been at the core of him since early childhood, when he had been orphaned. Even Aunt Marian's love had not been able to remove it. Sometimes his heart had leapt at a friendship but the friend had always gone away or betrayed. Never had an offer of friendship called up in him such a surge of joy and gratitude as he had felt at F.J.'s outstretched hand this weekend. Now it had been withdrawn.

F.J. had kept his promise to sleep upon Richard's problem; and the only answer he had to give Richard was the empty injunction to forget it. Well, Richard reflected, each of us is alone with his troubles. When other people give counsel they are generally as much concerned to evade becoming involved with us as to help us. And why not? Why recriminate? Everywhere that F.J. went, Richard told himself, he must be assailed by people who wanted to burden him with their problems, proposals and requests. If indulged they would take away from F.J. the time of his days and the use of his mind. F.J. must have his own share of troubles; and his mind must be all the time a-buzz with his own dreams. What else could he do but keep importuners like Richard at bay?

Richard hated to whine or to blame others for his griefs. One of his selves, however, entered a plea in his defence. It was not he who had sought the friendship. F.J. had by many tokens and encouragements invited his confession.

He turned in his walk, to wander back towards the high stone garden wall, a segment of which was framed in the end of the pergola. He paused. In that frame was one of his pictures, and it seemed only appropriate to him that it should have appeared at this time. It was The Man In The Mud. Richard went closer, as he might to a picture on a gallery wall. Its details became clearer.

The Man In The Mud was the most frequent of his visions. He knew the scene in detail. But this was not the picture as in earlier appearances. The scene was the same but it was portrayed from the opposite direction.

He now looked across the desolate landscape as if he were the enemy who had killed The Man In The Mud. The thicket of barbed wire was in front of him. The dead soldier who had fallen upon it now faced Richard. His head was held up by a strand of wire under the chin. His fair hair was a ragged thatch, dull as withered straw. His open eyes that saw nothing looked at Richard.

What Richard saw left him curiously unsurprised. He was looking at his own face. The dead soldier was named Richard Latt.

He stood still for many moments until the picture had vanished. He was unsurprised because the revelation confirmed and clarified vague intuitions that had troubled him. He had a sense of things falling into place, of all being right and proper. He was at last relaxed and peaceful. His doubts were resolved, his questions answered. Perhaps, even, there would be no more pictures. Why should there be? It was over. He remembered the name of a spot at which he had stopped for tea when he was on a walking tour near Loch Lomond. Rest And Be Thankful.

Later, in the same peaceful mood, he walked past the back of the house and came to the west garden. He heard voices from upper rooms of the house. People had gone up to wash before an early luncheon. He did not want to go inside yet. Portia was in the garden, too, on her accustomed seat near the pond, reading her book. He smiled at her but strolled on, not checking his pace. She smiled back and returned to her reading.

He turned left into the tall-hedged path that led to the river and the wood. He did not notice F.J. sitting in an arbour, writing in a small notebook. F.J. saw Richard. He put his notebook away and went after him.

Fifteen

Richard crossed the footbridge and walked among the trees. He stopped to pluck a leaf from the balsam poplar. He rubbed it between two fingers. He turned at the sound of footsteps and waited for F.J. to come up.

F.J. stopped at his side, uttered a sigh and remained silent. When Richard spoke it was in an indifferent tone. He was not much concerned about F.J.'s presence. Life had changed for him since his vision in the pergola. He said, "Are you really going to put it in a book?"

"No. It was just something to talk about."

Richard looked away. F.J. said, "It was wrong, I suppose, but you invite me, you seek me out, all you people. You must take me as you find me."

"Yes." Richard spoke placidly.

"Do you ever ask yourself why some people get on and some don't?"

"I don't think I ever have."

"I know writers of talent who haven't got on. You have to be as much dedicated to getting on as you are to writing. It's a matter of imposing yourself. Claiming attention. Second nature. I do it without thinking."

Richard said gently, "I do understand."

"It's only talk. It'll be forgotten. You needn't worry."

"I'm not worried."

"Tell me—" The new tack came abruptly. "How

come that a boy like you talks about life as something to be endured?"

"Endured?"

"You said on Saturday night that there were a few people who thought it worth while to endure life— It's not a view one expects from a boy of twenty-two whose lack of experience has been conspicuously demonstrated."

Richard said, "Oh—" and looked away again. At length he said, "Experience—" and pondered again. "I was taken away from my parents when I was five. A year later I was told that they were dead. Aunt Marian's awfully good to me. Well – I just have known since the moment I was told of my parents' death how frail and terrible the human state is."

"I see— And all that reading, I suppose."

"I suppose so."

"And you went to live in a settlement among the slums. I suppose that's experience."

"I have always been alone," Richard said. "Since I came to England. In spite of kind friends and relations. That must do something to one."

"Only a certain kind of person remains alone. You certainly are a deep one."

Richard did not respond. No more was to be confessed. After a while he said, "You know, I didn't think you would argue against me like all the others."

"Why not? I have a part to play. Dear boy, I am a performer." Richard looked at him, puzzled. "Yes, pundit, clown, it's all the same thing. Do you know what I really think? I think you haven't seen half the truth."

"Haven't I?"

"Not a tenth. And you may thank God for it, since you believe in Him. I am a visionary and I see things that make me want to die. I am the real visionary. My stories – the worst of them – are not jolly notions, wheezes to turn a penny. They are my dreams. And they're only the iceberg tip of my dreams. I dare not put the rest into words."

"What dreams?"

"You've had a glimpse of them. The tiniest glimpse. I see everything going wrong. Everything. My whole being is pervaded by an obsession with death. Death, death, death. We talk of change and our friends are all good people whose mission is to instigate, initiate, direct the courses of change. They are all so sure that it is a march to the light, without end. Beyond each horizon of progress another will come into view. But all consequences beyond the immediate are unpredictable. Shall I write stories, then, of a time of plenty when the machines, as we reformers predict, will do all the work for us, and man, freed according to our hopes from degrading labour, comes to regard all labour as a degrading invasion of his natural right to idleness? Shall I write about a civilisation threatened by angry hordes from without and reduced to chaos by the rush for the swill trough within? Shall I examine the problem of freedom and show what happens when it is pursued to infinity? Oh, that is only a glimpse of my reveries and speculations."

"And you think it better to conceal them."

"My boy, I have to. I refuse to live in hell, and you must not."

"I don't think I shall."

"You must wage your struggle in your way, I in mine. It is the central struggle of my life, the motive of all my present and I dare say future work – to suppress what I

186

have seen, to deny it to myself, to find arguments that will disprove it. Now you know why I am the great optimist."

"Yes."

"And of course – let us be a little cynical – it's the paying way."

"I suppose it is."

"I have been exorcist to millions. Few really believe in God any more, you know, so they need me. Even my horror stories purge them of deep fears by turning these fears into entertainments. And now I have gone on to preach and reassure. I drown my own fears by shouting my nostrums in the market place. I propose solutions to all the problems of mankind. The newspapers print them and pay me a lot of money for them, I am glad to say. I speak at banquets. I dine at great houses where I bestow balm as a priest bestows blessings. Call me the High Priest of the secular age."

"I see."

"And it all brings comfort to me. I need it, my boy. I need the flattery of statesmen and grand ladies, the honorary degrees, all the rest of it. Getting on is my means of survival. The enjoyment of a sort of power is my opiate. And all those girls who throw themselves at me – my dear Richard, I need them, too, every one of them." A sigh. "So you see, it was naïve of you to think that I would back you up."

"Of course."

"But all this does not lighten your burden."

"I'm all right. Really I am."

"You are a person of a rare sort and a rare depth. Can you banish the truth from yourself?"

Richard smiled. "Really. I am all right."

"My dear boy," F.J. said. "My dear, dear boy." He

placed a hand on each of Richard's shoulders and looked into his eyes. Then he drew the young man to him and, as closely as an Englishman dare, held him in an embrace. Richard wept softly. His father had embraced him so, at their last parting, when he was five.

F.J. left, without speaking again. Richard dried his eyes and stayed in the woods with his thoughts. Later, he went back to the garden. Portia was still there with her book. He went to her.

Sixteen

Portia looked up as he approached and put her book aside. He said, "Hallo."

"Hallo."

"I'm not mad, but it would all take too much explaining."

"I think it might."

"Portia—" He sat down next to her. "Do you think it would work if you and I married?"

Her scrutiny of his face was sombre. "You put it doubtfully. What's the idea? Do you mean to save me?"

"I'm not offering much, if your opinion of me is correct."

"You see us as two lost souls, perhaps, who might as well?"

"I would say possible partners. Helpmeets and all that."

"I don't see myself as a helpmeet."

"You can make a difference just being in someone's life."

"Yes," she said. "You see, I haven't turned you down with contumely."

"It's not easy to make myself understood. If I tell you what I want, it will sound as if I am making terms."

"What do you want?"

"I'd like to have a child. And I mean to go to India."

"What has India got to do with it?"

"My parents were there."

"I know. And?"

"I want to work there."

"What work can you do? You're trained for nothing."

"I'm strong. I can learn. My father's work was irrigation. He and my mother went into a district to get fresh water to some villages. They knew it was a cholera district, and they died of it."

"I don't understand you. Do you want to get cholera?"

"No. Just to work. Preferably in the same line."

"You must know," she said, "that I wouldn't meet either of your terms."

"I feared so. I'm sorry."

"Then why did you make the offer?" He was silent. She said, "If you cared for me, wouldn't you give up your conditions?"

"If I did, would you say yes?"

She considered him again. "I'm no use to you." He was silent and she said more strongly, "I'm no use."

"If you valued yourself more—"

"Anyway, you can't give up your terms, can you?"

"No."

"And I think you made the offer out of some notion that it was for my sake."

"No. But to be plain you are rather in a mess."

"And?"

"I hate to leave you."

"I would rather not be pitied. I shall have a good time, you know."

"All right." He stood up.

"It doesn't fit in," Portia said.

"What doesn't?"

"This about work. And a child, for heaven's sake. If those ideas of yours were true—"

"We have to live."

"Then you must be mad. According to you it's a waste of time."

"All life is, but we've got to decide how to live it."

She smiled, and said without rancour, "Little Jesus."

"Oh, no. I've not wanted to be holier-than-thou. I've proposed – well, I meant it."

"And I refuse. With thanks."

He stooped. She let him kiss her on the cheek. He said, "I shall see you in London."

"Oh, yes," Portia said. "And no blushes. But no more earnest walks in the Park, I fear."

"No."

In the afternoon the clouds blew away and summer returned. The sky was blue and the sun lit the earth with radiance. Richard walked out to the wicket in whites and cricket cap, bat under his arm, big ridged pads like a knight's greaves protecting his legs below the knees. He chose his position while the fieldsmen closed menacingly in upon him. He prodded down a bump in the grass, took guard and waited in a wary stance over his bat. The first ball came down. He hit it and ran.

From a distance – say, from the churchyard on the rim of the hill – the game continued with a slowness as of insects. The little white men stood still or made small movements in the middle of the field, one sometimes scampering after the ball while the two mannikins with bats scuttled to and fro.

On one side of the field the gentry sat at ease in front of the pavilion, their clothes making a pretty composition.

On the other side, the villagers were a noisy, jolly swarm around the marquee. The vast silence of rural England was faintly fretted by the yelp of an excited player, the rattle of clapping, the undulating murmur of voices, momentary bursts of laughter, the cries of children and the dull knock of ball upon bat.

It made a picture that was not like any of Richard's: a quilt of landscape in many colours, a small field in its midst alive with people and their pleasure, an old house close by with sunshine gilding its grey stones, the immense green barrow of Long Down lying behind, part of the long, low range of hills; the hills supporting an infinite English sky. God's in His Heaven, said the poet, All's right with the world.